Dream
Dimension

AE Moran

Invisible Publishing Company

Contents

Chapter 1: Juliet

I an Campbell puffs out his cheeks, sticks out his tongue, crosses his eyes, extends his hands at arm's length reaching for my throat. He lets his head flop to one side and his wild, floppy, dreadlocks make him look like a goggle-eyed monster. "Brains! Zeke the Zombie eats brains!"

I burst out laughing, cock my arms at strange ales, and lurch a few mechanical steps toward him without bending my knees. "Robot Rex! Scanning the area!"

The whole group of animators gathered around laughs along with us and Sophie Jennings pats me on the back. "Robot Rex was a sensation. You're a genius, Juliet!"

Ian straightens up and drops his zombie act. "Zeke the Zombie was a sensation, too. Give me some credit."

"Always," I tell him. "We can all be geniuses together."

I pick up my drink and Frank Butterfield pretends to look into my glass. "You aren't drinking brains for lunch, Juliet. What's the matter? Are you coming down with a cold?"

I join in the joke. "I need to hit the booze before I start canvasing this conference for Animatrix's future investors."

My fellow animators and I put the jokes on hold while we survey the surroundings. This is the first networking event I've been to that takes place in the grand ballroom of a luxury cruise liner. No one could ask for a nicer venue than the *Dream Dimension*. It's the other people in the room with us that spoil the atmosphere.

Frank wrinkles his nose at a bunch of corporate types schmoozing by the buffet table. "What's the nicest name we can call them?"

"Let's be diplomatic and call them conference attendees," I reply. "Maybe we can capitalize on this conference by turning some of these people into cartoon characters for our next sequence."

"Great idea!" Ian pulls his head so far down into his collar that his neck completely disappears. He crunches up his eyes and purses his lips before he starts staggering around bumping into things. "Corporate Carl is coming to suck your blood!"

The whole group bursts out laughing. "They aren't vampires," I point out. "Corporate Carl will suck the money out of people's bank accounts before he sucks anyone's blood."

"You have to feel bad for them," Sophie remarks. "Imagine having the bad luck to get stuck in a corporate job where you have to dress like *that*."

The other animators go back to joking around, but I can't help checking out the corporate people across the ballroom from us. They're attending the same conference, but they couldn't be more different from Animatrix's employee base if we all landed from different planets.

My employees wear casual clothes and Ian is even wearing a *Star Wars* t-shirt with a blazing floral Hawaiian shirt over that. Frank wears a Minecraft baseball cap turned sideways and black-and-white checkerboard Converse All-Stars sneakers that have been around since the late 1970s. No wonder none of the corporate people will come near us.

I did my best to wear the uniform. My plain, tight, navy-blue dress comes down to my knees, but not even I could blend in with the crowd of suits across the room.

I'm supposed network with these people, not hang out with my friends making up new cartoon characters for our next animation sequence. Animatrix might have a culture of fun and wacky humor, but I'm still the boss.

I'm the one who's supposed to pitch investors to scale this company and make it grow. I built this company from scratch and I'm responsible for keeping it afloat.

Ian reads my mind and claps me on the shoulder. "Go on, Captain Pioneer. Assemble your landing party and take your away team to the planet's surface. Bring back a full scientific survey on the native alien fauna so we can dissect them and study their internal organs."

I laugh, but not as heartily as everyone else standing around. That's my cue. If I don't go now, I'll never go at all and this company needs investors—not to mention new clients.

This is the part of my job I like the least, but it is part of my job. Ian gives me one last shove and I drag my heels over to the group at the buffet.

They see me coming a mile away and I'm as alien to them as they are to me. They move out of the way to give me a straight path to the buffet. It never once crosses their minds that I might want to talk to them—because I don't. I'm transparent to them.

I might have been able to blend in with them if I hadn't been hanging out with those freaks across the room. I might as well have, *Animation Geek,* tattooed across my forehead.

I pretend to take a carrot stick from the dip tray while I listen to their conversation going on behind my back.

"And then I said to him, 'If we can't get the balance sheet squared up by the end of the year, we might as well close our doors right now'," a man in a stiff, blue suit is saying. "The whole house of cards will come tumbling down without some third-party oversight."

"I completely agree with you," another man replies. "Where's the moral hazard? That's what I want to know."

I gather my resolve, take a deep breath, and turn around to introduce myself to them, but as soon as I lay eyes on them and their matching suits, shiny shoes, Rolex watches, and their slick silk ties, I can't go through with it.

I don't want to become like these people. I don't want to catch the corporate disease. Becoming like them would be my worst nightmare. What's the point of being an animator and running a company like Animatrix if I'm going to become like every other corporate slave on the planet?

I can just imagine the dialogue going on among my fellow animators as they watch me flee in defeat. I go over to the bar to get a refill on my drink. I'm going to need to top off my tank with booze before I build up the nerve to try to make these people think I'm one of them.

Two more corporate guys stand at the bar getting drinks, too, but I don't even look at them. Corporate people in suits are starting to haunt my nightmares. I really need to turn them into some kind of cartoon villain that someone has to fight their way through to reach a prize. That would make a really good animation sequence.

I bemoan my fate and start fantasizing about my office computer back at Animatrix headquarters while wait my turn to get my drink. I'm a million miles away when one of the other guys waiting turns to me and sticks out his hand.

"You're with Animatrix, aren't you? I loved your work on the Tip-Top Toys marketing campaign. That Robot Rex character was pure genius!" He bursts out laughing, angles his arms downward from the elbow, and moves his head from side to side on his neck in a mechanical way. "Scanning the area!"

I laugh and shake his hand. "Yeah, thanks. Guilty as charged. That was me."

"I'm with Chase Manhattan Bank, so I probably wouldn't have any use for your service, but I know a lot of people in marketing. I'll definitely drop your name if it ever comes up."

"Thanks," I mutter. Great. The one person who knows about my business and thinks it's good isn't in any position to help me promote it.

He shakes my hand again and takes himself off somewhere before I realize that I didn't even get his name. I'm an utter failure at everything networking.

I turn back to the bar feeling even more defeated when the second guy standing there turns to me. "Animatrix.....you're on the list of businesses seeking investment."

I barely look up. "That's right."

The bartender comes over with my drink and I take a gulp. I can't face the room to go back to networking. Maybe I'll just stay here and drink myself into an early grave instead.

"I'm Damian Mitchell. I'd be interested in investing in your company."

It takes me a second to realize that the guy is still here. He's talking to me of all people.

I look up and almost turn my back on him when I see his immaculate black tux. He's dressed way better than every other office slave in this room, but he doesn't flaunt it with the diamond Rolex and gold cuff links. He keeps it understated with just the tux—which is plenty.

Short, brown curls top his head and bright green eyes latch onto me when I look up at him, but something in those eyes puts me off. They don't twinkle or flash with any kind of hidden light. I've been hanging around animators for too long. I've developed a sixth sense for people who have no sense of humor at all.

This guy might fill out a tux nicely with square muscular shoulders, chiseled arms, and a trim, narrow waist, but those eyes tell me all I need to know about him.

He sticks out his hand to me the way everyone is supposed to stick out their hands at these events. I realize a second too late that I'm looking at like it really does belong to some alien monster about to attack me.

I manage to shake his hand trying not to look too disgusted. "I'm Juliet Holloway. I'm the CEO of Animatrix."

"So tell me about your investment profile. I hear Monahan Marketing tried to acquire Animatrix last year and you barely headed them off before they succeeded."

I jolt to high alert and stiffen. The guy stands in front of me gazing back at me with that direct, inscrutable stare. Now my spider senses are definitely tingling.

"Are you interested in investing....or acquiring?" I ask.

He shrugs. "I don't know. I guess I would have to find out more about your investment profile.....which is why I asked."

"If you're trying to acquire Animatrix, I'm not interested." I toss back the rest of my drink and put my glass on the bar without slamming it down as hard as I'd like to. "I built this company from nothing and Animatrix is not for sale."

"I didn't say anything about buying it," the guy counters. "You're here to pick up investors, aren't you?"

I glare at him. Everything about him sets my teeth on edge. The fact that he looks like a corporate version of James Bond only makes me mad. "Investors," I fire back. "I'm not here to meet anyone who wants to acquire my business."

"Why not? A business is only worth the sale price."

My eyes fall out of their sockets and I stare at him in horror. He did not actually say that about Animatrix—my company, my passion project, my baby.

I would never sell Animatrix and anyone who thinks they can acquire it against my wishes. Anyone who thinks that is definitely not someone I want to be talking to at a networking event or anywhere else.

I turn away. "It was nice to meet you. I gotta go. See you later."

I hope I don't see him later and I can't go back to networking after this. How many other people here might be trying to steal my business out from under me?

I cut a wide path away from the rest of the Animatrix staff. I don't want to talk to anyone right now. I want to go back to my cabin, take off this dress, and relax.

Stopping Monahan Marketing from pulling a hostile takeover on Animatrix was hard enough. I lost months of work pulling out all the stops to prevent the takeover and it probably took five years off my life. I can't go through that again.

I don't get out of the room without the Chase Manhattan guy from the bar introducing me to three other people, but I barely hear them before I make my escape. I head down the corridor toward the elevator.

Next time I attend a networking event like this, I'm going alone. Bringing the rest of the Animatrix staff will only distract me and bringing them along doesn't endear me to the people who might invest in my business.

I hate thinking about my employees as a shameful secret I need to keep hidden. Our fun, joking culture is what makes Animatrix great. We sit around firing off jokes and ideas all the time. Our headquarters office is an aquarium of playful creativity. That's how we come up with some of our best ideas.

I love my business and I don't want to change it, but I'm responsible for selling it to the people who understand it the least. It's a delicate balancing act I don't always pull off as well as I should.

I owe it to my animators to make this company work. We're family and I could never let anything happen to them. They're the ones who made this company as successful as it is and I really let them down tonight.

I slink off toward my cabin and I kick off my high heeled shoes in the elevator. Who am I kidding? I'm just a kid at heart like all the rest of my staff. I don't belong in a tight dress surrounded by office zombies in suits.

I relax against the elevator wall, and by the time it dings on my deck, I'm ready to crawl into bed and forget that tonight ever happened. I step out into the corridor and make it halfway to my room when a devastating crash strikes the ship from one side.

The impact hurls me across the hall and I bang into the opposite wall. Screams, the crash of breaking glass, and gut-wrenching tearing sounds rock the ship as the floor tips sideways.

Room service carts, shattered crockery, and bodies slide across the carpet and slam down all around me. People scream and claw at each other trying to grab hold of anything they can.

I flounder in panic trying to figure out what's happening when another brutal crash echoes through the ship. What the hell is going on? I can't see anything but terrified people and piles of debris all over the place.

Another deafening bang makes the light fixtures sway and more sounds of breaking and tearing come from every direction. I can't figure out what's going on and then the ship groans back the other way.

Everyone screams as we all go tumbling across the corridor. People slam into the other wall and try to scramble out of the chaos to stop themselves from being thrown somewhere else.

I grab onto a table, but it isn't fixed to anything, and a second later, another blow flings everyone into the air. I catch a moment's glimpse through a nearby porthole and my heart stops.

Flashing lights illuminate the ocean outside the cruise liner. Another ship angles its prow into the *Dream Dimension*. The two ships must have crashed into each other, but that doesn't help me.

The next instant, I crash down hard on the floor and try to blink the stars out of my eyes. I barely have time to figure out where I am when another excruciating wrench yanks the floor out from under me.

I somersault head over heel as the whole ship leans sideways. I try to grab hold of the carpet, but there's nothing here to hold onto. I pitch back the other way, slide through an open door, and sail across what looks like a bedroom cabin.

I hit the other wall and scream again when a chair and a bunch of debris land on top of me. I curl in a ball trying to protect myself, but a second later, everything goes quiet. The ship stops moving.....and so do I.

I pant hard to catch my breath and slowly uncurl my arms to look around. The room is leaning hard to one side and the floor slants up at a forty-five-degree angle to the door high above me.

I crawl painfully onto my hands and knees gasping and groaning in fear and agony. I have to get out of here somehow, but when I take another look around the room, I freeze again. I'm alone except for one other person. It's the guy from the bar—Damian.

Chapter 2: Damian

I drag myself to my feet and spot a woman couching on her hands and knees nearby. I stagger over to her, but it isn't easy with so much crap clustered around my feet and the floor tilted at a steep angle.

I balance in the channel between the floor and the wall and stumble over to her. "Are you okay? Are you injured?"

She looks up panting hard through bared teeth and I see that it's the woman from the bar—the woman who got offended when I mentioned investing in her animation company. What did she say her name was? Oh, yeah. Juliet. Juliet Holloway.

She doesn't look so put together now with her long, straight dark hair saturated in some nameless goo. Her dress is torn and bruises and scratches cover her face and arms. Other random stuff sticks to her dress and she's barefoot.

Her brown eyes blaze with a different kind of fire and she barely sees me. Her petrified gaze darts around the room and she rasps with every breath.

I squat down next to her and lay my hand on her shoulder. "It's going to be okay. We'll get out of here. Just tell me if you're hurt anywhere. Do you need to go to the hospital?"

"I'm....I'm.....okay....." she gasps. "I'm.....okay."

I take hold of her arm. "Can you stand up?"

She doesn't fight me when I try to pull her to her feet, but as soon as she stands up, the boat lurches again and she topples against the wall. I fall, too, and I wind up falling on top of her. I barely get my arms into position on either side of her shoulders to stop myself from crushing her.

She screams, but I can hardly blame her. "What's happening!" she shrieks.

"Hold on!" I yell. "We're going over again!"

The boat groans a little farther over on that side before it stops.

"Jesus!" I choke. "We gotta get out of here!"

"How?" she yells. "We can't get to that door, and even if we did, the whole boat will be like this. We'd be in the same situation no matter where we go."

She isn't saying anything I haven't already thought of. I roll off her and lie against the tilted wall trying to think. She's right. The whole boat will be in chaos. "Maybe we should just stay here."

"We don't have any choice," she fires back.

She's being so sensible that I glance at her again. She might be a mess right now, but she's just as level-headed and alert as she was in the bar. She picks up minute details much quicker than anyone I've met in a long time.

She tries to push herself off the wall. "There has to be something we can do. Maybe there's another way out of here."

"I doubt it. Look." I nod toward the windows nearest us. They give a full, sweeping view of the ocean outside. "The boat is listing away from us. We're hundreds of feet above the water. We're better off staying here."

She collapses against the wall, shuts her eyes, and swallows hard. "This is not my idea of a pleasant evening's entertainment."

"I didn't mean to offend you earlier when I asked about acquiring your business."

Her eyes snap open and she spins around to stare at me. "Well, you did offend me. Animatrix isn't for sale."

"Sorry. Most people who start a business want to sell it someday. You're the first person I've met who wouldn't sell for the right price."

"No price would be enough. I didn't start this business because I want to sell it. I started it because I love what I do and I want to keep doing it."

"Okay." I raise both hands. "Are you still looking for investors?"

She eyes me with suspicion. "Don't pretend you want to invest if you really want to steal my business out from under me."

"I don't steal."

"You mentioned Monahan Marketing. You might be thinking of pulling another hostile takeover."

"Can you blame me? Animatrix has a well-deserved reputation in the industry."

"What industry? You never mentioned what business you're in."

I frown at her. She's the first person I've met in years who doesn't know who I am. "I'm Damian Mitchell. I'm the CEO of Masters Marketing."

Her jaw drops and her face drains of all expression. She gapes at me in....well, I have to admit she's gaping at me in horror. Most people are thrilled to meet me and I have to drive off entrepreneurs with a baseball bat. They all want me to acquire their businesses from them.

Not her. She doesn't like meeting me. This is a first.

Master Marketing has a well-deserved reputation in the industry, too, but she doesn't fall over herself telling me what an honor it is to meet me. She looks like she wants to run screaming from the room, but that isn't possible.

She pulls it together and goes back to looking around, but there's nothing to see that we haven't already seen. Stacks of broken dishes, overturned potted plants, tangled sheets, and pillows saturated in coffee lie strewn at our feet.

A single overturned queen bed lies at an angle in the corner, but we can both see that it doesn't reach as high as the door. We can't get out of this room.

She pushes herself off the wall with another exasperated gasp. "Do you have a phone? We could call someone."

"Oh, yeah. I didn't think of that." I pull my phone out of my pocket. "There's no signal, but I might still be able to call 911."

I dial and the operator comes on the line. "911 Emergency Dispatch. Please state the nature of the emergency."

"We're on board the *Dream Dimension* in the middle of the harbor!" I tell her. "We're trapped in a room on Deck 15 and we can't get out!"

"Emergency crews are already on scene, Sir," the dispatcher replies in a bored voice. "EMS is already doing everything possible to right the ship. Is anyone in your immediate vicinity in life-threatening danger or does anyone have critical injuries?"

I glance over at Juliet, who watches and listens from a few feet away. "No. We don't."

"Then I can only advise you to stay where you are until EMS arrives. We're fielding calls from all over the ship and life-threatening injuries will get top priority. If anyone suffers serious injuries or your situation worsens, you can call us back and I'll divert services to your location."

I hang up. "So much for that."

Juliet starts rummaging in the piles of stuff at our feet. "Maybe there's a way to rig up some of these sheets and climb up to the door."

"You mean like a prison break in reverse? Good luck with that."

She whips around fast and her hair goes flying. Her eyes bore into me with plenty of their old stony intensity.

All at once, she straightens up, angles her head at a bizarre tilt, cocks her elbows in a comic way, and jerks right and left. "Scanning the area!"

She bursts out laughing and I scowl at her. "What are you doing?"

"Nothing. Forget it." She drops the act and goes back to wading through the debris. "Why do you want to acquire Animatrix anyway? You don't get our sense of humor."

"I run a marketing company. I need animators."

"You could hire Animatrix as a client. You don't need to buy us out."

"I prefer to have executive control over all my company's output. I find that the numbers stack up better when I keep all creative output in-house. I can control outgoings by offering other types of compensation such as stock options or benefits. It helps our balance sheet and gives me more control over the company's image through the work we put out."

She snorts and turns away. "That's what I thought. You're all business. You don't understand what makes Animatrix unique."

"Of course I do. What makes it unique is how successful it is. Animatrix is one of the few animation houses still operating independently."

"And you want to change all that, don't you? How do you think we got where we are? We don't let anyone control our creative output and we never will. We like Animatrix the way it is.....but you wouldn't understand that. You have no sense of humor."

"I have enough of a sense of humor to realize that the customers love your work."

"But you don't love our work. You don't connect with our playful attitude. Everything is a numbers game to you."

"That's business."

She turns away again and I catch her making faces while she keeps her back to me, but she doesn't answer. She starts pulling sheets out of wreckage. I don't see what she's going to do with them. She wouldn't be able to tie them to anything in this reverse prison break she's planning.

I look out the window and a chopper crosses my line of sight. At least EMS is on the way. We won't be stuck in here forever—at least, I hope we won't.

I push myself up and start moving toward the overturned bed when another crushing boom rocks the ship. The whole boat pitches sideways, topples in the opposite direction, and slams down hard on the windows right next to my head.

The impact hurls me and Juliet off our feet. We slam into the other wall near the door and then go flying back to where we were as this side of the boat hits the water with earth-shattering force.

All the windows explode and a devastating torrent of sea water rushes into the room. It slaps me and Juliet out of the way and carries us both across the room.

I get sloshed in a churning cauldron of sharp edges, spiky wooden splinters, and ice-cold water. I flounder to get to the surface, but I can't even tell where the surface is.

I flail, break the surface, and bump into a body. I try to grab hold and Juliet screams as the current tears her out of my grasp. "Juliet!" I roar. "Where are you?"

She starts to scream again and gets muffled by another dowsing wave pouring into the room. I break the surface for a split second, just long enough to see a massive wall of water crashing straight for me.

It smacks me hard against the wall and I go down choking on a mouthful of water. I get tumbled in all directions until, like something out of a distant dream, strong hands grab me by the jacket and haul me out.

I gag and splutter before I realize that Juliet is pulling me sideways. She lands against the wall where we were before and all the water sloshes away from us.

I collapse gasping and spluttering for every precious lungful of air. Juliet lies saturated and drenched at my side with her arms still wrapped around me. My petrified brain won't switch gears.

"Are you all right?" she gasps. She starts patting me down. "Did you get hurt?"

"I'm.....I'm....okay......." I turn to look at her. "Are you all right?"

She nods and her wild eyes dart around the room. The ship is back in its previous position with the now-destroyed windows towering over the sea. I don't trust myself to move in case some other disaster strikes.

"That was....close...." she croaks.

"Yeah.......Thank you......" I can barely get my voice working. "I owe you big time for that one."

She looks over at me and our eyes meet. She really is incredibly beautiful in a deeply genuine way. The water dripping from her hair and skin only makes her look more appealing. Another trick of fate might kill us both in a few seconds. If I'm going to die....why not?

I lean and kiss her. She doesn't try to stop me, and when I ease back to look into her deep brown eyes, they burn with a different kind of fire. She's thinking the same thing I am.

I lunge for her and she comes at me with the same ravenous passion. I attack her mouth kissing her fast and hard. I want to disappear into her and feel as much mind-destroying pleasure with her as I can for as long as it lasts. I want my last moments to be nothing but her.

She launches herself at me just as hard and starts yanking my jacket to get it off. I can't touch her fast enough and I grab one of her breasts. She moans into my mouth and rises on her knees to climb on top of me.

I tear into her dress, but it's too tight and stops me from touching her the way I want to. I slide my hand up her thigh and push her dress up as she slings her leg over my lap.

She arches her chest into my hands and moans when she rocks down on my hips. She wants this as much as I do. We both want to forget all about where we are and what might happen to us any second now.

She strips off my jacket and goes to work on my shirt buttons. I shove her dress up and burrow both my hands into her panties. I squeeze two big handfuls of her ass and pull her tight against my crotch. God damn, she feels good!

Her body sways in time to my rhythm and she grinds her sweet box against my throbbing bulge. Hell, yes. This is so perfect.

She gets three of my shirt buttons open and slips her hand against my chest. Her touch sets my blood on fire and I bite down on her lip. She squeals and I pull off to dive into her neck.

She moans and sobs when I mouth down to her chest, but I still can't reach the rest of her. She pulls away long enough to slide down the zipper on her dress and she shoots me a wild, electric, crazy grin when she pulls her dress over her head.

She rises before me looking glorious in her bra and panties. I have to have her. I sit up and scramble onto my knees with her perched on my lap. I yank down her bra cups and take a big mouthful of her breast.

She screams when I start to suck, but this is a whole new kind of scream—the kind I love to hear and can't wait to hear again. She arches back in my arms convulsing and spasming on my hips as I drive up into her. She can feel how hard I am and she loves it.

She rips my shirt off without trying to unbutton any more of it. She pulls it over my head and her wicked little hands light my skin on fire when she touches me. Her velvet arms stroke my back and she glides down my spine to squeeze my ass.

I can't stand being away from her mouth and I rise up to kiss her. Her eyes transform with ecstasy and ravenous insanity when I flick her bra open.

She shrugs out of it and leans back to take hold of my belt. The feeling of her unbuckling my belt drives me to the stratosphere and I yank at her panties.

She kisses me again and inches backward just enough for me to get my fly open. That's all I need and I groan when her hand closes around my shaft. Holy fuck, she's so fucking hot!

She comes at my mouth again, and before I know what hit me, she sits down on me and we lock together in an unbreakable bond. Her eyes tell me something so much deeper and our bodies move in timeless rhythm that nothing can break. I almost hope the ship sinks right now so this will be the last thing I ever feel and see and experience.

Her hot, throbbing flesh clamps around me and she starts riding me like I can't believe. My body takes over and I match her rhythm moving with her. She hangs onto me as her eyes slip out of focus and her eyelids droop with so much rapture that I can't stand it.

I kiss her while we rock and sway in an unending rhythm. Christ, she feels so good! I cradle the back of her neck in one hand and she melts to my direction. She relaxes in my arms even as her body tenses to the breaking point with rising energy.

I ease her back and buck into her driving her to the stars. She winces and screams until I pull her in to kiss her again. Her hair falls over me and her face shines with so much pleasure that I can hardly control myself.

I will myself to hold this rhythm, but she's flying out of herself too fast. Her excruciating cries spike to screams and her muscles ripple and clench around me. She's going way too fast.

I dive in and grab her breast in my mouth. Her fingers thread into my hair and she hugs me into her chest. Her other hand rakes my back, around my shoulder, and against my chest. Her touch gives me superhuman strength and I pull back to feast my senses on her magnificent face.

Her head wobbles on her neck. Her eyes drift shut and then snap open to drill me ravenous, animal madness. She intoxicates my senses with every moan and facial expression. Her lips shiver when she sucks air through her bared teeth. My God, she looks absolutely feral like this!

I try to kiss her, but she's so out of her mind that she doesn't respond. Her body feels heavenly in my hands and I press against her lower back to push her down against my thrusts.

She screams, and when I try to ease off, she doesn't stop screaming. She arches back, shrieks to the ceiling, and then collapses against me whining and sobbing as her body explodes around me. Her sweet honey gushes around my shaft and her head falls on my shoulder.

I kiss the side of her head as she screams in my ear. I try to fight myself under control, but the power of her climax sets me off and I plunge into her with all my might. I hold onto her for dear life as we both float away into blessed delight.

Chapter 3: Juliet

I sit on the edge of my desk and flip through a few pages on my tablet. "How's the Casaba Coffee sequence coming along, Frank?"

Ian cuts in from the back of the room. "Frank is writing himself into the sequence showing an old guy drooling down his shirt while he drinks Casaba Coffee."

The whole staff explodes with laughter, including Frank. "That's right, pal," he calls over his shoulder. "Whenever I have to look across the office at your face, I drink Casaba Coffee and I instantly feel better."

"Are you putting Ian in your sequence, too?" Sophie interjects.

More jokes, insults, and rude remarks fly around my office and I raise my voice to holler over the noise. "Okay! We're supposed to be having a business meeting here, people! I asked a question, Frank. How's the sequence coming? I don't want to know what the sequence is or who's in it or how many times you drool down your shirt."

Everybody laughs. It takes way too long for Frank to get a big enough break in the mayhem to answer me. "It's coming along fine. I should have it done by Friday."

"That's perfect. That's a week ahead of time. Can you top that, Ian? How's the Children's Hour opening title shaping up? Are you a week ahead of time?"

"Hell, no, he isn't!" Sophie cuts in. "How can you even ask that, Juliet? He'll be lucky if he's two weeks behind schedule."

"Maybe you need to drink some Casaba Coffee," Frank calls out.

Everybody laughs and I have to wait way too long to answer. "Stay behind for a minute, Ian. We need to revise your deadline."

"Who said anything about a deadline?" he asks. "I'm an animator, not a journalist."

"If you're more than two weeks behind schedule, you need a deadline. The rest of you can skedaddle."

"Skedaddle!" Frank remarks. "I'm going to add that to my sequence."

"You're a week ahead of schedule so you can do what you want," I tell him.

"You hear that, Ian?" Sophie calls. "Get ahead of your schedule and you can do what you want."

"I do what I want anyway," he replies.

Everybody gets up talking, laughing, and teasing on their way out of my office. We didn't get as much done in that meeting as we should have, but we never do. Meetings are more an excuse to get together and shoot the bull. We almost never actually accomplish anything. We save that for our desks.

Ian waits until everyone else leaves and then slopes up to me. "Don't give me a deadline, Juliet. You know I can't handle pressure."

"Finish the Children's Hour title by Monday morning or I'm going to take it away from you. Your timeframes keep falling farther and farther behind. We aren't here to play all day, Ian. I'm actually trying to run a business here, and if I don't get paid for the work you're supposed to finish, *you* don't get paid."

His jaw drops and the color drains from his face. "You don't mean that."

"Do you think I went to that networking event because I enjoy rubbing elbows with suits, Ian? Do you think I went because I went because I have nothing better to do with my weekend? I did it to scare up investment in this company. If we don't finish our projects—and by that I mean on time—none of us gets paid. This company will go under and we'll all be out of a job, including you. If you can't pull it together, you're out. This is your last warning."

He stares at me with his mouth open. "You wouldn't...you could n't.....we're....we're family!"

"So I should let the rest of the staff starve on the street because you can't handle your timeframes? It's you or the rest of us, Ian. It's as simple as that."

He stares at me in such horror that my heart twists. I hate acting like the boss with any of my employees, but he doesn't give me any choice.

I sink down in my chair and bury my face in my hands. I hate this and I hate the way he's looking at me. I wish my job was nothing but jokes and fun, but it isn't.

I force myself to look up to see tears welling up in his eyes. I wave toward the door. "Get out of here, and please, for the love of God, go back to your desk and get to work on that title. Don't talk to anyone or joke around or play video games. Just do your job. Please."

He doesn't move. I knew this would hit him hard, but it's just as hard for me.

I stand up and go over to him. I touch his shoulder. I want to hug him, but something tells me to keep some professional distance between myself and my employee—just this once.

"Listen. I'm sorry. I don't like this any more than you do, but I'm leaving here to go to a meeting with a potential investor from the conference. It's a miracle we got this one after the accident, but I have to go because this company needs investors. That's my job—to make sure our bottom line stays healthy enough for all of us to stay employed. I need you to help me with that. I need you to put as much effort into this as I do. That's all I ask. I'm not running a charity here. This is a business, and if I'm pulling eighty-hour weeks and spending my weekends making this company work, you can do the same thing."

He opens and closes his mouth a few times, but he doesn't answer before he finally gulps and leaves the room. Damn it. I don't want to lose Ian, and if he thinks I was too hard on him, he might just quit. This company's culture of fun and play is one of the main draws that keeps such talented animators working here.

I'm not running a daycare center, though. They do actually have to work.

I heave an almighty sigh and bend over my tablet. I have to put Ian out of my mind and concentrate on this meeting. I need to be bring my A game so I can get Sorenson Commercial Image Management on board as an investor. I can't let them slip through my fingers. I need this too badly.

I run through a few documents on their business and then change my clothes before I drive across town to the meeting in their office tower conference room.

I check my appearance in my rearview mirror and then again in the car window before I go inside. I actually look somewhat like a business executive and less like a dopey animator that someone decided to let out of the zoo.

I chuckle at that idea on my way into the building. I'm going to have to use that one in a sequence, too. I'm full of ideas and I just can't help myself from coming up with zany images and animation sequences off the top of my head. Animatrix's culture has a way of influencing my every thought. All my employees are like this, including Ian.

Maybe I could have gone easier on him. He's one of my best animators. He's just pathetic when it comes to sticking to a schedule. He's too creative to be much good with anything business-related.

I pull my head back to the matter at hand when I step out of the elevator and walk down the hall to the meeting room.

One of the receptionists leaps up when I get near the door. She hustles over to open the door for me. "Go right on in, Ms. Holloway. The negotiating team is waiting for you."

I smile back at her. "Thank you."

This is promising. The negotiators must be as excited as I am to get their investment in my company.

The door swings back, stride into the room, and all my excitement and enthusiasm drains out through the soles of my shoes when I see Damian Mitchell sitting on the other side of the table.

I recognize three other people from the board of Masters Marketing. What the holy fuck are they doing here?

Everyone on the other side of the table stands up and Master Marketing's vice-president extends his hand to me. "Thank you so much for coming down, Ms. Holloway. We're delighted to get this meeting started."

"I....uh.....I thought I was meeting Sorenson Commercial Image Management. No one said anything about Master Marketing." I make a deliberate point of not looking at Damian. He's behind this. I just know it.

"Sorensen is a subsidiary of Masters Management," a woman at the end of the table tells me. "Naturally, the governing board of Masters Management has to get involved with any acquisition negotiation."

"Acquisition!" I don't even try to keep my voice under control. "This is not an acquisition! Your contact said you wanted to invest in Animatrix."

"We do," the vice-president tells me. "We're willing to offer twenty-five percent above the spot stock price to gain a controlling share of....."

"No damn way!" I blurt out. "No one is buying out Animatrix! No way! Never in a million years!"

The woman waves to the chair across the table. "Please sit down and we can discuss this, Ms. Holloway. I'm sure we can come to some mutually agreeable number."

"No, we can't!" I snap and I find myself addressing my outburst only to Damian. He sits silently through the whole confrontation, but I can just feel his insidious tentacles slithering through this whole disgusting confrontation. "There is no number you can put on Animatrix that could possibly induce me to turn over a controlling share of the company I built from the ground up. If you really want to acquire Animatrix, we're done here."

"Be reasonable, Ms. Holloway," the vice-president tells me. "A company is only worth the sale price. I'm sure you'll agree that...."

I don't stick around to hear anymore. I storm out of the room and slam the door—or I try to. The hinges catch its weight so that it glides closed softly and gently. That just makes me even madder than I already am.

The bastard! Damian did this. He sucked up to me during the *Dream Dimension* accident, hooked up with me, and then went behind my back to try to acquire Animatrix against my wishes.

I fucking hate him. I could gouge his eyes out, but I have a much bigger problem. I need investors, and on top of that, now I have to deal with another potential hostile takeover.

I may not run in corporate circles, but I know enough about Masters Marketing. If they want to acquire a company, they get it.

They have a scorched-earth reputation in the marketing field and that approach to business must come from the very top.

Damian. He did this. He maneuvered himself into my pants and now he pulls this shit. Bastard. Fucker. Asshole.

I'll stop him. Animatrix means too much to me to hand it over to a snake like him. This company is my baby. If I had to sell it or see it go over to someone, it definitely wouldn't be him. He doesn't understand humor or fun or play or any of the things that Animatrix stands for.

I have to stop him and that means I need to scramble to find some other investors—serious investors. I need to find people who want to save Animatrix as passionately as I do and I need to find them fast. I need to find them before Damian cuts me off at the pass. My whole future and my staff's livelihoods depend on it. I can't fail.

Chapter 4: Damian

I turn from my computer and flip through the prospectus for the Network Entertainment public offering. I compare the numbers from the prospectus to the numbers on the spreadsheet and find an error. That isn't good. The Network Entertainment finance department better not be flubbing the numbers or I'm going to have to bring the hammer down.

I scroll through the rest of the spreadsheet on the alert for any irregularity when I hear footsteps coming close to my office from outside. My ears prick up. No one should be in the building at this hour. Everyone besides me has already gone home for the day. I'm the only one hardcore enough to burn the midnight oil this late at night.

I keep scrolling while I listen to the person getting nearer. They're really walking fast and not making any effort to keep quiet. I freeze to my chair when my office door flies off its hinges and a woman storms in.

She plants herself across my desk and my nerves tighten when I recognize Juliet. I would have to be blind not to see the blaze of fury in her eyes and the tight pinch to her lips.

"What the fuck do you think you're doing trying to buy out Animatrix? I told you on the *Dream Dimension* that my company is not for sale. Who the fuck do you think you are trying to cut me off at the knees?"

I try to stay calm, but I have to fight the urge to stand up. She's so irate that she actually look scary like this. "No one is trying to cut you off anywhere. We made you a very generous offer...."

"You offered to steal my life's work! You offered to take the blood, sweat, and tears that I worked for and throw it on the trash pile of history in exchange for a handful of money."

I take my hand off the mouse extra slowly so she won't think I'm making any sudden moves. I never expected her to react like this. "You don't understand, Juliet. You are probably the only business owner any of us has ever met that wouldn't want to sell their business....."

"Do you think I give a fuck what kind of business owners you've ever met? Was I speaking Chinese when I told you on the *Dream Dimension* that I didn't want to sell Animatrix?"

"It's a business decision," I tell her. "We would be foolish to...."

"You did this!" she spits. "You were the one who directed your board to steal my company."

"I brought Animatrix to the board's attention, yes."

"I knew it!" She slams her fist down on my desk hard enough to rattle all my computers. "I never should have trusted you. You son of a bitch! You took advantage of me when we were alone on that boat...."

I lower my voice to the danger zone. "I most certainly did not take advantage of you. Don't you dare even suggest that. What we did was totally consensual...."

"I'm not talking about that, you jackass!" she roars. "I'm talking about my business! You saw my name on the list of businesses seeking investment and you said you wanted to invest. You never said anything about a hostile takeover....."

"It isn't a hostile takeover if you just accept our offer....."

"I told you that ANIMATRIX IS NOT FOR SALE!! What part of Animatrix is not for sale did you not understand?"

I shrug. "Business is business. If you offer shares on the open market, anyone can come along and buy them. If they're there for sale, we can buy them. You can't legally stop us."

She narrows her eyes at me and I have to will myself to hold her gaze. She looks ready to attack me. "You bastard!" she hisses through gritted teeth and trembles with rage. "You are the last man alive that I would ever let take Animatrix from me. You will never lay a finger on Animatrix as long as I'm alive to stop you."

I do my best to shrug again, but she's so furious that I'm losing the courage to argue with her. This is definitely the first time I've ever had a confrontation like this in all my years in business. "If you can scrape up the money to stop me, more power to you."

She glares at me and shivers all over holding back her fury. "Scrape?" she snarls. "*Scrape* up the money? You fucking, worthless, heartless, bloodless son of a bitch!"

I take a deep breath and get to my feet. I can't let this go on. I have to stop this before it gets any worse. "Look. I thought I was engaging in a mutually agreeable business transaction. I never thought you would react like this. If I had known....."

I trail off. What would I have done if I had known? Most of the time, when someone says their business is not for sale, they mean the offer price is too low. Who in their right mind would balk at selling their business for significantly more than its market value? It's unheard of.

She moves a step back like she expects me to get violent with her or something. Her eyes go insane with fury and hatred.

She flares her nostrils drawing another shuddering breath. She's so enraged that she keeps her voice low to a deadly murmur. "You and your...you board.....don't have a fucking clue what my business is about. Your company is the absolute last thing in the world that I would want Animatrix getting involved with. You think you can take Animatrix and suck it up under Masters Marketing's umbrella and everything will just go on as before? Is that really what you think?"

"Why wouldn't it? You run a good business. Anyone can see that."

She shakes her head and turns away. She won't look at me again. "You don't know what you're talking about. You don't know the first thing about my business."

"I know your reputation for excellence. I've seen enough of your finished work...."

"My business is not about the finished work!" She rounds on me spitting tacks. "My business is about people having fun—and making the audience happy. My business is about infecting humor and happiness and enjoyment into everyday life....and making people laugh. Do you even know what it means to laugh?"

"Of course I do. That's why we want Animatrix—because of the way it makes people feel. That's exactly what we want for our marketing."

She stares at me for so long that I'm not sure she even heard me. She finally snaps out of it and jolts. "You will never get the quality of work from Animatrix if you carry out this takeover. I'll take all my best animators and leave if you don't drop this plan right now. I'll gut the company and leave you with nothing."

"You can't do that. You'd be obligated under the terms of the...."

She chops her hand through the air and starts to turn away again when her eyes slip out of focus again. She reels backward, staggers, and almost falls over. Her hand flies to her head and she groans.

"Juliet?" I ask. "Are you okay?"

She lurches sideways and I leap forward to catch her as her knees buckle. "I don't feel so good....." she mutters under her breath.

"Come over here and sit down." I steer her toward a chair by my desk.

"I....don't think.....I can't see."

I look around at nothing, but when I try to pull her toward the chair, her legs completely give out and she falls to the floor. I barely tighten my grip on her in time to stop her from completely collapsing.

I lower her the rest of the way to the floor and try to roll her onto her back. "Juliet! Juliet!"

She groans again and doesn't answer. I have to do something to help her. I lie her down flat, lunge for my desk, and grab my phone. I dial 911 and rush back to her side fighting down the urge to panic.

"911 emergency dispatch," the operator chirps. "Please state the nature of the emergency."

"We need an ambulance right now!" I roar. "I'm at....."

"Damian....." Juliet's eyes drift open and she looks up at me, but I can't tell if she even sees me. Her face is as white as a sheet and her lips tremble. She doesn't look mad anymore. She looks terrified. I get a flashback to the *Dream Dimension* disaster. Is she about to die?

"I'm right here, baby," I tell her. "I'm right here."

"Damian......" She swallows hard and her hand floats toward me. "Don't leave me....."

"I'm right here." I grab her hand. "I won't leave you."

"Sir?" the operator asks. "Are you there?"

"Yes!" I yell. "We need an ambulance at 482 Cityscape Parkway! A woman just collapsed in my office. She's on the floor and she can't stand!"

"I'm dispatching an ambulance now, Sir. Please stay on the line until emergency crews arrive."

The operator asks me a bunch of other questions that I barely hear. I can't stop staring down at Juliet. She keeps drifting in and out of consciousness, but she never lets go of my hand. She crushes it in a death grip, but I don't care. I never want her to let go.

The ambulance crew rolls into my office and tears me away from her. My hand and my heart and everything else feels empty, now that I'm no longer touching her. Nothing better happen to her. I couldn't live with that if me trying to buy Animatrix caused this.

The paramedics surround her doing and asking a million things at once. I can't think straight until I get in my car and drive to the hospital. I have to be there for her. I have to find out what happened, and if there's anything I can do, I have to do it.

Chapter 5: Juliet

I shiver under the blanket and try to concentrate on not flying apart at the seams. I keep spinning off into semi-consciousness, and when I do come back to reality, I feel like I'm going to pass out at any second.

I keep my eyes shut so I won't see Damian sitting in the chair by my bed. I need someone here. I just wish it wasn't him. I wish he wasn't seeing me like this. He probably thinks I'm weak and that will make it easier to steal Animatrix from me. Dream on, sucker.

I can't think about that right now or I'll really start to freak out. I have to find investors to prevent this hostile takeover and I can't do that if I'm flat on my back with whatever deadly disease I'm coming down with.

He works on his phone while we wait for the doctors to give us the bad news. He keeps looking up and he stares deeply into my eyes whenever he sees me looking around the room. That's all the more reason to keep my eyes closed.

Some part of me is secretly grateful that he's here....and that he was there when I collapsed. He handled it a hell of a lot better than some of my colleagues at Animatrix ever could.

That's one thing about working with a bunch of creative types. I'm the one who handles things. I'm their surrogate mother. I'm the one who deals with the real world so they can float off into their fantasy lands.

He isn't like that. He can deal with reality. If he had a humorous bone in his body or even knew how to play a little, he would be perfect—except for the fact that he wants to steal Animatrix from me. I'll never forgive him for that.

He's a heartless, humorless, lifeless cadaver. He cares more about what's on his phone than he cares about anything else.

That isn't true. I can see that from here. He spends a lot more time looking at me than at his phone. He only goes back to it when I shut my eyes.

I gulp and try to turn away, but I'm too emotional right now. I need.....someone. I just wish......

I jump a foot in the air when one of the nurses pulls back the curtain around my bed. The woman doctor who interviewed me when I first came in steps up to my bed and consults her clipboard.

"Well, the blood test results came back positive, so there's nothing to worry about."

"What do you mean—they came back positive?" I ask. "Positive for what?"

"You're pregnant. You're about four weeks along, so you're right on schedule with all these hormonal fluctuations. They'll pass as soon as you reach about twenty weeks."

I gape at her in stunned disbelief. "I'm.....what?"

"You're pregnant. If you'd like to stop by the pharmacy on your way home....."

"I can't be pregnant!" I practically shriek. "I'm on birth control. I have the patch. I've never....."

"Every method carries the possibility of failure. Don't worry. The patch won't adversely affect your pregnancy, but it is important that you take it off as soon as you get home just in case it causes problems later on....."

I barely hear the rest. She rattles off a bunch of instructions, but only two words stick in my brain. I'm pregnant.

My eyes flick over to Damian. I'm four weeks along. That means......

I lean forward and start pushing off the blankets. I have to get out of here, but I'm still so weak that every move costs me a massive effort. I need to go home. I need to get away from Damian. I need to think and plan and....everything.

The doctor finally gets me to sign the release paperwork and I put my feet on the floor. I try to get my brain working while I gather up what few possessions I had with me when I went to Damian's office.

The doctor and the nurse finally leave me alone and he comes over to my side. His presence makes me want to puke. "Well, that's good," he murmurs. "You can get it taken care of and no harm done."

"Get what taken care of?"

"The pregnancy. You can end it and go right back to work. It won't mess up your life....or mine."

"You.....actually think I would end it? Do you have a drop of blood in your body? How could you even suggest that?"

He shrugs. "I'm just saying. This could have been much worse. As it is, you can put it behind you and it doesn't have to interfere with either of our careers."

I stare at him. He's really the most heartless, lifeless clod I ever met. I finally shake my head and push him away. "Go home. Leave me alone."

"I can't. I just told the doctor that I would give you a ride."

"You what?!" I shriek.

"Didn't you hear me? She asked if you had any way to get home and I said I would drive you. What do you think you're going to do—walk? I don't think so. Look at you. You can't even stand up."

I blink at him as my brain switches back into gear. He's right. I don't have any way to get home and it's too far to walk even if I was in perfect condition.

The only other option is to call someone from work. My mind immediately switches to Ian, but I can't call him after reprimanding him earlier. He's probably at his desk working on the Children's Hour title right now.

I can't call anyone else from work, either. I don't want any of them to know about this—not yet.

Damian takes hold of my elbow and starts helping me stand up. "Listen. I'll drive you to the appointment and pay for it and everyth ing....."

"I'm not ending this pregnancy. I'm having this child whether you like it or not."

"So you would destroy my life along with your own? Thanks a lot."

"My life won't be destroyed. I've always wanted children even if I have to have them with an asshole like you."

He purses his lips and sighs, but he still doesn't lose his composure. Does anything touch this guy? "Be reasonable. How do you think you're going to manage your career with a kid around?"

"That's my business. I'll see you later. Call me when you're ready to see sense."

He hovers around waiting, but when I finally get out of bed, get dressed, and pull out my phone to call a cab home, he gets the message and leaves.

Chapter 6: Damian

I stroll up to Animatrix's office door and pause to take in the scene. A bunch of people in what look like Halloween costumes slouch around at their computers, yell back and forth to each other, and one guy is even lobbing popcorn into another guy's mouth.

I'm just about to check out the big white-board roster schedule by the door when a young woman happens to pass me. She doesn't notice me at first and then pulls up short. She scans up and down my body and her eyebrows fly up when she sees my suit. "Are you lost or something?"

"No, I'm not lost. I'm here to check out your company."

She frowns. "Do you have an appointment? Does Juliet know you're here."

"No, she doesn't know I'm coming." I stick out my hand. "I'm Damian Mitchell."

She glances down at my hand and backs away. "I think you better talk to Juliet about this."

She makes it five feet before she hollers over her shoulder. "Juliet! Some dude is here!"

Juliet's voice drifts from out of sight. "Who is it?"

"Not sure! Some guy in a suit."

Those words ricochet like a shockwave through the office and everyone looks up from what they're doing. Now I can see why someone in a suit coming here would be so unusual. These people have never seen a suit in their lives and forget about wearing one.

No one moves for a second until Juliet comes out of her office. She walks around the corner laughing about something behind her and goes ice cold when she sees me. "What the hell are you doing here?"

"I'm here to check out your business."

"Well, you aren't welcome here. Get out of here before I have you arrested for trespassing."

"Your shareholder information statement says that any shareholder can inspect your premises, work undertaken, and employee conditions at any time. I'm a shareholder so I'm here to see what you're doing and how you're doing it."

She narrows her eyes at me. "You aren't a shareholder. You're trying to acquire this company through a hostile takeover."

"I'm a shareholder as of this morning." I pull out my stock owner's certificate and hand it to her.

She studies it and then scrutinizes me. "Don't think you can get away with this. I know what you're trying to do."

"I just told you what I'm trying to do. I want to see what you're working on and how you run this operation. You don't have to assign malicious motives to it when we haven't even gotten started."

"Fine." She hands the certificate back. "I think you should come into my office so your presence doesn't disrupt the employees."

"Okay." I scan the place again. A few people keep gaping at me like I dropped from another planet, but most go back to work as Juliet leads me to her office.

A sloppy, unshaven character with shaggy dreadlocks and a *Jurassic Park* t-shirt is busy making faces, sticking out his tongue, and making goggling noises to the people nearest him, but he stops instantly when sees me watching him.

He drops back into his chair, hunches over his computer, and doesn't look at me again. A hush falls over the room that definitely wasn't there when I first walked in. How can one man's presence have such a profound effect on these people?

Juliet waves at the room lined with computer stations. "As you can see, this is our work premises. Each animator has their own station set up to their own preferences and specifications depending on the work they do."

"Show me some of the projects you've been working on."

She scowls at me for a second and then leads me the rest of the way into her office. "You can sit down here." She quickly swipes away whatever was on her computer screen and moves her tablet out of the way.

She clicks her mouse a few times and pulls up completely different documents so I don't get to see what she was just working on.

Her desk is much better organized than any of the freaks out on the floor. She has a pen mouse in addition to a regular computer mouse. A large grid pad covers most of her desk. I guess that's for her to do her computer drawing on.

She moves out of the way to make room for me to reach her chair. "This is a schedule of all our current projects. You can click on the title and it will take you to the submitted work the animator has completed so far. The links in this column will take you to all the documentation of the client requirements and any preliminary design documents the project is based on."

She steps back and I sit down. I click on the top entry and it opens a video player. It starts playing an animated commercial for Casaba Coffee showing a cartoonish character drinking his coffee, rolling his eyes in ecstasy, and sighing in delight.

It ends with the character tipping his head way too far back on his neck, opening his mouth to a huge size, and dumping gallons of coffee down his neck before rocketing away, bouncing off the walls, and finally exploding out the window into the clear blue sky.

I burst out laughing at the comic genius of the sequence. I click on another entry that shows another video of a children's show opening title. This one has a whole bunch of cartoon zoo animals dancing and prancing across the lower part of the screen. They bounce and twist and contort in silly dance maneuvers that make me laugh again.

The letters for the *Children's Hour* TV show hop and dance and squirm across the screen higher up. They look like they're bopping along with the animals. The animals across the bottom get more fantastic and outrageous as the title goes on.

Eventually, monsters, mythical creatures, and some I've never seen before make their appearance, but they're all so cute and obviously having so much fun with their wacky dance that none of them looks horrible or scary. They just look like they're having tons of fun.

I get so engrossed in what I'm looking at that I forget all about Juliet until she moves across my line of sight. She stands across the office watching me with her arms crossed over her chest. I can't read her expression, and as soon as I look up at her, she walks out of the room.

I turn back to the schedule. This stuff is gold. I've seen plenty of Animatrix's work before, but this is really pushing the limit of creativity. The company's reputation really is well earned.

I scroll down scanning the animator names on the schedule. I don't recognize any of the names until I get halfway down and spot one with Juliet's name next to it.

I click on it and a long line of windows comes up. Some are sketches. Some are fully drawn-out pictures and some are snatches of very basic animation.

The sequence tells the tale of one Little Boy Jake traveling through a fantasyland of obstacles, strange creatures who try to stop him from going any further, and a few friendly characters who help him. I scroll farther down the timeline and find out that Little Boy Jake is on a quest to reach the Mountain of Mystery.

Juliet's sketches of the mountain at the end are shrouded in clouds, and when Little Boy Jake reaches the top, he finds a treasure chest that spills rainbows everywhere and makes him unimaginably happy. He takes the treasure chest back down the mountain to his family and lives happily ever after.

A prickle goes up my scalp looking at the happy family at the end.....and then I scroll back through all the images and sequences of obstacles and creatures the character has to overcome.

The truth hits me like a lightning bolt in the brain. This is life. It's a fable about struggling to find happiness in life.....but the schedule doesn't list any client name that might have ordered this project.

Juliet must be doing this on the side. She must be making this film sequence for her child. I run back through it examining every detail. Her drawings are childlike, hilarious, and extremely appealing. I can see how this would be the perfect vehicle to teach a child about persevering in life and finding the mystery treasure on top of the mountain.

Maybe having a kid wouldn't be so bad after all. It might actually be fun if a kid had a mother like Juliet who took the time to share the child's playful, innocent experience.

That picture and the sequence infects my mind with all kinds of ideas, but a second later, Juliet comes back and I instantly click away from the project. I open something else so she won't see me looking at it.

She plants herself across the desk. "Did you find what you're looking for?"

I look up at her and I have to smile. If I have to have a kid, I'm glad it can be with her. She's creative, feisty, smart as a whip, and very determined. She'll make this child a very good mother.

She said she always wanted children. She'll be delighted to have this child, which is good for the child. I wouldn't want this child to have a mother that harbored any resentments or doubts about what she was doing.

What about me? I wouldn't want this child to have a father that harbored any resentments or doubts about having a child, either. No child should have to put up with that.

That puts me in a curious position, doesn't it? This is my kid. I'm going to be the other parent in this kid's life. If I don't want this child's father to have any resentments or doubts, then I can't have any resentments or doubts.

I find myself beaming up at Juliet. I really need to make this work with her, even if neither of us asked to get into this situation. "Yes," I tell her. "I found what I'm looking for."

"Does that mean you're ready to pack up and leave us alone."

"No, I want to see a few more of these projects. I'll tell you when I'm done."

I turn back to the computer and she takes her tablet out of the room. I check out a few more of the projects on the schedule, but a second later, an icon pops up at the bottom of the screen. The desktop synchs with her tablet to show what she's working on.

I click on it and it opens a proposal document to Paper Tiger Film Studios. It includes the schedule I'm looking at as an attachment. She's pitching the studio to become an investor for Animatrix.

I have to grin at the language of her proposal. She specifically highlights Animatrix's independence as the basis for its creative genius. She makes certain to point out that the company will remain independent so it can continue to deliver the best possible content to the audience that appreciates it the most.

Touché, Juliet. She's talking about me. She wants to secure the company where I won't be able to get it. That's okay. I can respect that.

I hear Juliet coming back and quickly close the document so she won't know I saw it. I go back to checking out some of the projects. She works on something else and doesn't interrupt me until I finish.

I finally stand up and close the schedule. "I'm done. I'll get out of your hair now."

She snorts. "As if that's likely to happen."

I spread both hands. "Look. I know I'm not the guy you wanted to have kids with, but we're in this for the long haul now. We might not like each other, but we're having a kid together so we have to make it the best it can be. We should work together to make this child's growing up experience as positive as possible. We should cooperate and communicate with each other about what's best for this child. What do you say?"

She glances over her shoulder toward the wider office floor when I mention the child. She must not have told any of her employees yet that she's pregnant and she'd be loopy to tell them about me.

She eyes me suspiciously and then shrugs. "All right. I can't argue with that."

"Great. Why don't we meet on Saturday and discuss where we're going to go from here."

"Saturday....when? Please Dear God tell me you aren't trying to ask me out on a date."

"Of course not. We're just going to talk and hammer out how we're going to proceed with this whole co-parenting operation."

"Fine. Just make it in the afternoon and not at night."

"Okay. No problem. What time would you like to do it?"

"Two o'clock. I'll meet you at the Oak Street Kitchen."

I can't help but grin at her. "Perfect."

She studies me across the desk and I look back at her. My attitude toward her and this pregnancy has just turned a corner. I think I can get on board with this now. If her animated film can do that for me, it could do wonders for a wider audience. She really is an incredible person.

Her eyes give me so many crazy ideas that I can't tear myself away. I get another flashback of our time on the *Dream Dimension*. She's beautiful and passionate and brilliant, but she also hates me. That isn't going to make for a very successful co-parenting relationship. That's going to have to change.

"Are you finished?" she finally asks. "Have you seen enough?"

"Yeah, I have." I look away with difficulty. "I'll see you Saturday."

Chapter 7: Juliet

I cringe when I see Damian sitting at a table at the Oak Street Kitchen. It's two o'clock in the afternoon, but this definitely feels like a date.

The café is empty except for the two of us. Sunbeams slant sideways through the windows and casts long shadows across the table. The whole scene looks......well, romantic.

That's the last thing I want it to be, but I'm already here and Damian has a point about us cooperating to co-parent this child in the best possible way. I should have been the one to offer that olive branch, but he did it first. Maybe he isn't such a bad guy.

I walk over to the table and try to keep it businesslike when I sit down and put my handbag on the floor. "Hi."

"Hi." He starts to stand up and then sits down at the same time I do. "Thanks for coming."

I spread my hands and take a deep breath. "I should have offered to cooperate with you sooner. I apologize for my attitude."

"You don't have to apologize. I understand why you would feel hostile when I asked you to end the pregnancy. I didn't understand at the time why you wanted to keep it. I thought you were too driven and career-oriented....like me."

"Well, it's done now so let's get on with the subject of how we're going to do this."

"It's pretty obvious, isn't it? I'm this child's father and I want to be involved as much as possible. I want to be there when the kid is born and....."

"What?!" I snap. "You want to do what?"

"I want to be there when the kid is born and I want to be there for your doctor's appointments and ultrasounds and...."

"No way!" I blurt out. "You aren't going to my doctor's appointments and you definitely aren't going to be there when the baby is born."

"I have to be. I'm this child's father. What do you think—that I'm just going to stand by and let you push me out of this child's life? Forget it. I'll take you to court if I have to."

I stare at him in mounting horror. This is not happening to my child. No way in Hell. He isn't going to come into my life and start throwing his weight around.

He compresses his lips, casts a glance around the café, and leans across the table. "Look. This is not what I meant by cooperating. We can't turn every conversation into an argument."

I look away. What was I just saying about being the one to cooperate first?

He leans back, turns sideways, and picks up a black nylon zippered folder from the chair next to him. He hands it across the table to me. "I'd like you to take a look at these and tell me what you think."

I don't know what to say except to yell at him. He is NOT going to my doctor's appointments. Fuck that.

I take the folder not thinking anything of it. Anything is better than wherever it is he wants this co-parenting thing to go.

I unzip the folder, open it.....and my mind goes blank when I stare down at a picture drawn in colored pencils. The shading and pencil strokes are so perfect and well blended that it takes me a while to figure out exactly what medium they're in.

I stare at the top sheet and I would have to be blind not to recognize Little Boy Jake, but someone has redrawn my original character. The face is more expressive—and funnier. It's more ridiculous and comical.

I turn over the first sheet and then flip through a bunch of the scenes from my sequence. The scenes are more complex and deeper and whoever drew these pictures has expanded on them and added a few idiosyncratic behavioral movements to Little Boy Jake. They look like screwy dance moves kind of like the ones from Ian's Children's Hour title, but these are totally unique. I've never seen them before and I burst out laughing, they look so silly and charming.

I come to some of the obstacles and antagonists that Little Boy Jake has to overcome to reach the Mountain of Mystery. A few additional creatures and monsters occupy different positions in the sequence. Some are scary and some are just downright gut-bustingly funny.

The second one is a race of creatures known as The Squares. They're dumpy blocks with legs and screwed up faces that make them look like they're always frowning. Each one wears a tie and they look suspiciously like the corporate people from the networking event on the *Dream Dimension*. I can't tell the difference between the males and females and their expressions are beyond priceless.

"Where did you get this?" I ask while I turn a few more pages. "This is incredible."

"I drew them. I want you to incorporate them into that film of yours.....and I think this is a more compelling version of Little Boy Jake, don't you? The other one was kind of bland....not that I'm saying anything against your character. I just think some of the lines in the face could have been more distinctive."

My head snaps up. "You drew these? How?"

"I did a lot of art when I was a kid. That's how I got into graphic design, but once my business took off, it made more sense for me to hire other designers to do my graphics for me. I had to concentrate on actually running the business so I let it fall away." He nods at the sheets. "What do you think?"

"This is....." I can hardly speak and my eyes keep skimming over the pictures. He did this?

How could I ever think he didn't have a sense of humor? The body movements he's added to Little Boy Jake are over-the-top comical and The Squares.....

My eyes flick back up to Damian's face. He gazes at me across the table and I see him in a whole new light. He's more than funny. He's creative and insightful. He would have to be to turn his own corporate coworkers into such a perfect humorous representation of them.

"What's the verdict?" he asks again. "I know it isn't as good as some of the stuff your team puts out, but if you like it...."

"Like it!" I gasp. "This is genius! Why aren't you an artist?"

He laughs and his cheeks color. "Maybe I should be."

I can't stop turning the pages. His changes flesh out the story much more thoroughly than I could have. He's enhanced some of the other characters and landscapes to make them better defined and more appealing.

"Anyway," he begins again. "I want you to add these to your film. My kid is going to see this, so I want to have something to say about the content."

I raise my head and blink at him. My kid? Did he just say that? Is this the same guy who wanted me to end this pregnancy?

He fidgets in his chair and glances to one side. "You're making me nervous. Could you answer my question? Do you think these are good enough to incorporate into your film?"

"Oh! Sorry. Yes. They're good enough....and yes, I will incorporate them. Do you....?" How do I put this? "Do you want to let me know if you have any other changes you want to make?"

He bursts into a huge grin. "I'd love to."

My brain switches gears and I almost ask him if he has any other input to make to any of Animatrix's other projects, but I catch myself in time and don't ask that. He isn't part of Animatrix....but maybe he should be if he can come up with something like this.

I glance down at the pictures. "Are you okay with me taking these back to the office? I can copy them and then return the originals to you."

"That's okay. You can keep them. I have others at home."

My jaw drops. "You do?"

He blushes again and looks down at his hands. "Don't tell anybody, but seeing your projects kind of....woke up the sleeping dragon, shall we say? I haven't picked up a pencil in years, but after I got home from visiting your office, I kind of.....exploded. I drew those....and a bunch of other stuff."

I can't stop staring at him. This guy is an artist. He's more than an artist. He could be.....he could be anything. He's definitely talented enough to work for Animatrix. He's even better than Frank and that's saying something.

I do my best to get my head screwed back on straight. This is the guy that got me pregnant. He wants to come to my doctor's appointments and be there when the baby is born.

Those requests don't sound so insulting and outrageous now. He's thinking about this baby as his kid. He wants to be involved, and if he's coming up with drawings for my film, maybe he's actually serious about being a father.

"I....uh....." I stammer. "I'll incorporate these and then send you the sequence so you can see if you want to make any other changes."

"Thanks." He smiles at me across the table and his eyes sparkle with something I've never seen before. He was so wooden at the conference....and then......

I realize in a heartbeat that I *have* seen that look before. He looked at me that way while we were doing it. That's the most alive I've ever seen him.

What if he could be like that all the time? What if he *is* like that all the time and I just don't know him well enough to see it? What if I've been so hostile to him all this time that I didn't let myself see it?

He's always had to defend himself against me.....except for when we were alone in that room together. It came out then....and now.

He looks around again and shifts in his seat. "Look. You're a professional animator. I'm nothing. Maybe...you'd like to.....come back to my place.....and take a look at some of the other stuff I've done....."

He slides his hand across the table and his fingers close over mine. A bolt of lightning rushes up my arm from his touch. Is he suggesting....*that*? It isn't like I can get pregnant again because I already am.

I know I'll enjoy it, so why not? Relations between us can't possibly get any more complicated.

He tugs my hand and nods toward the door. "Come on. Let's get out of here."

Chapter 8:
Damian

My heart starts to race leading Juliet to my car. She doesn't speak nor does she try to take her hand out of mine on our way across the street. I open the passenger door for her and she slips into the seat.

She looks straight ahead and doesn't say anything when I get behind the wheel and drive across town to my apartment building. I can't believe we're actually going to do this again, but after the way she reacted to my drawings, why not?

I park in the underground parking garage and switch off the engine. I glance over at her at the same instant she glances at me. Her dark eyes gleam with the same fire I saw on the *Dream Dimension*. She wants this. She's already getting excited. She gazes up at me with big, wide, glistening eyes.

The instant I make eye contact with her, she looks down at my mouth. She's thinking about it, too.

I lean in and kiss her and the chemistry between us explodes off the charts. It's like we're back on the *Dream Dimension* except that our lives aren't in danger and we both know exactly what we're doing.

She kisses me back just as passionately, and in a second, she wraps her arms around my neck and leans into me. Her tongue lights me on fire and I can't stop touching her.

She's wearing jeans, a t-shirt, and a short leather jacket so I can't reach much of her like this, but that doesn't seem to matter.

I slid my hand between her legs and she moans when I squeeze her. She rocks against my hand and rides my fingers when I rub the seam of her pants. Fuck, yes, I remember exactly how this feels!

She does the same thing, crawls her hand up my leg, and massages me through my pants until I throb for her. I can't stop kissing her, and when I clench my fist in her hair, she relaxes into my grip.

This is going way too far too fast and I don't want to do this in the car. I pull away, and without saying anything, I get out and go around to her door.

She gets out without looking at me or talking to me. I take her hand and lead her to the elevator. We stand there not talking or making eye contact while we wait for the elevator to come.

The doors ding open and we both step inside....and attack each other kissing, touching, squeezing, rubbing, and breathing hard.

She shoves her body against me moaning and mewling when I crush her sweet box through her jeans. She comes at me so hard that I stumble into the wall. She presses her weight against me and I feel myself starting to lose control.

I pivot her around and pin her to the wall mauling every part of her that I can touch. I want to take her right now, but at that moment, the elevator dings again.

I straighten up and she clears her throat when I take her hand again. I lead her out into the corridor, unlock my apartment door, and let her in.

She takes a minute to check out the apartment. She wanders into the living room and surveys the cityscape stretched out beyond the windows. She strolls along the windows gazing at the rooftop terrace, the hot tub, the pool, and the patio surrounded by trees.

I wait for her to turn around, but she doesn't. She just stands there staring until I call, "Over here."

She jumps, spins around, and then follows me into the other room. I lead her into the dining room where all my drawings from the last couple of days lie spread all over the table. None of them are of the Mountain of Mystery storyline. I separated those out to give her.

She bends over them and combs her hair behind her ear checking out the characters, the landscapes, and the scenes. She smirks at a few and then her cheeks color when she laughs. I guess I did something right.

I find myself studying her profile and observing the parade of emotions and impressions crossing her features. She's beautiful and talented enough that her opinion matters to me. It's a massive victory for me that she thinks my work is good enough to incorporate into her film. I'm not just making marks on a piece of paper.

"Do you always use colored pencils?" she asks me.

"Pretty much. I tried a few different kinds of paint, but none of them ever worked out as well as pencils. I always just kept coming back to this. It seems to work for me."

"It definitely does." She moves around to the other side of the table. "I never knew colored pencils could be this expressive." She laughs again when she points to one big landscape scene with some stylized animal characters interacting. "This is priceless! How would you like a job as an animator?"

Now it's my turn to blush. "I think you have enough staff and I already have a job."

She looks up and grins at me. "Let me know if you get fired or anything."

"Do you want something to drink?" I ask. "We never did get around to eating anything at the café."

"Sure. That would be great."

I leave her bent over the table and go out to the open-plan kitchen on the other side of the living room. I'm pouring two glasses of juice when she wanders out still smiling.

She puts her handbag and my folder on the living room coffee table and goes back over to the windows. "This is pretty impressive, but I guess that's what you get when you're a big-shot CEO like you. You have the whole world at your fingertips."

"It isn't all it's cracked up to be. I realized after leaving your office that I really am missing something living here by myself."

"You mean....?"

I hand her the glass. "I mean I didn't realize that I wanted kids until you insisted....and then when I saw your film......I don't know. I guess I never really realized what could be possible....or how it would affect my life. You were right about that, so.....I'm sorry I asked you to end it. I should be thanking you for sticking to your guns."

She breaks into a huge smile and her eyes shine. "Is that you're way of thanking me?"

I have to laugh and my cheeks flush. "Thank you."

She saunters down the line of windows and takes a sip of her juice. "It's hard to imagine a child living like this."

"Why?" I sit down on the couch and prop one foot on the coffee table. "It's as good a place as any."

"I just never imagined anyone living like this.....except a lonely, lifeless Square."

I burst out laughing again. "You got me."

"How did you come up with the idea? I didn't think any of your kind would be able to see it for its comic value."

"My kind? Ouch."

"Hey. I thought of it, but you're the one who actually put pencil to paper and did it. What changed?"

"I don't know. After I left your office and went back to mine....I couldn't stop seeing it. They're all so.....so Square."

She laughs, comes over to the couch, and sits down, but she makes sure to sit far enough away that I won't be able to touch her. Is this how it's going to be for the rest of eternity—us keeping our distance from each other except when we both break out and can't keep our hands off each other?

"What do you think you'll do, now that you've woken the sleeping dragon?" she asks.

"I don't know. Maybe I'll start covering the walls in art. I really don't know what's going to happen, but something definitely will."

"You could save covering the walls in art for when you have a kid."

I glance over to find her looking at me with that look again. She doesn't fume and snap at me. This is the most amicable conversation we've ever had and she doesn't balk at me talking about doing art with my kid.

Her eyes catch me in that hypnotic tide I can't escape. I just want to keep falling deeper and deeper into that bottomless pit of unstoppable intensity.

I'm still floating in that mysterious world when she leans in and kisses me. Our breath and lips and faces merge, but I still swim in the vast sea of what an incredible person she is as our bodies come together again.

Her tongue tastes unimaginably delicious and her breath blows my mind. I want so much more than just a quick fix like the one we shared on the boat.

She eases back and smiles at me the way she did at the café. She actually looks happy about being with me.

I comb my fingers through her silky hair. "Let's go upstairs," I whisper.

She doesn't respond except to smile at me with that overpowering look in her eyes. I stand up, take her hand, and lead her to the stairs up to my bedroom.

Chapter 9: Juliet

I don't know what to do with myself when Damian leads me into his bedroom and shuts the door behind me. He still holds my hand like we're coming home from our date at the café. Is it possible it's turning into *that* between us?

I keep telling myself not to let him into my life. I still want to be independent, but when he stands before me and gazes deep into my eyes, I can't remember why I want that.

My body feels different, now that I'm pregnant. It almost feels like my body recognizes the man who got me pregnant and I respond to him in new and unknown ways.

He starts kissing me, but it isn't the ravenous mauling attack of either of our previous sessions. He doesn't tear my clothes off and plunge in the way he did on the *Dream Dimension*. He doesn't claw at me and get me all worked up the way he did in his car.

Those memories make me so fucking hot that I can't help but ache for him. I want to do it with him again, but it feels different this time. My body almost wants him to implant this baby in me. I want to somehow make it official that he's the one who fathered this child.

He doesn't rush, though. He just stands there kissing me and letting me wrap my arms around his neck. He feels how tense and excited I am for him, but he just stands here savoring that feeling and looking into my eyes.

I can't hide from that look. He sees me for all that I am and I want him to see that. I can't believe I didn't know how talented he is. I'm finding out for the first time who he really is on the inside. I didn't know on the *Dream Dimension*.

He eases back, straightens up, and smiles down at me from above. He looks genuinely happy that I'm here in his room and we're about to do it. His cheeks shine and his eyes flash with inner light. When did he become so....so alive? He was never like this on the *Dream Dimension* or afterward....but maybe he was and I just never saw it.

He takes hold of my jacket and I shudder when he pulls it off. He does everything with agonizing slowness and deliberate care. He takes an eternity to lay my jacket aside and then he kisses me for another long, deep, luscious age before he snaps my bra clasp behind my back.

That sensation sends a shockwave through me. He's doing it. He's going to take my clothes off and then he'll see my body in ways he never has before. He'll see me in the light of day and not in a mindless rush.

He doesn't stop kissing me while he pulls my bra straps down my arms on both sides. Now my bra hangs loose with nothing holding it on. He reaches under my t-shirt and pulls it out....and that's it.

He goes back to kissing me while I stand before him braless. My shirt excites my nipples so I quiver all over with anticipation.

He finally decides to step back and starts unbuttoning his shirt. "Take a seat," he tells me.

I sit down on the edge of the bed, but my gaze keeps migrating up to him. He just keeps smiling down at me like this is the happiest he's ever been in his life.

He strips off his shirt and I get an eyeful of the body I remember from the *Dream Dimension*. He's just as cut and muscular as I remember, but seeing him like this with all the time in the world to appreciate him only makes me ache for him even more.

He comes over to me, kisses me, and then pulls my t-shirt off over my head. He won't stop kissing me as he tips me over backward onto the bed.

His skin feels soft and inviting when I lace my bare arms around his neck. I can touch his back and shoulders and chest as much as I want as he crawls up onto the bed on top of me.

He kisses me down flat and lowers his body on top of me. Damn, he feels so good! I never thought it could be like this between us. I thought we would just keep being hit-and-run joy toys to each other.

His eyes tell me something very, very different as his rock-hard body pulses on top of me. I can't deny the iron hardness between his legs and he keeps pumping into me until I moan, but he doesn't take it any further. He doesn't take his pants off nor does he try to take my jeans off.

After a long, succulent time of that, he rolls off onto his pillow, pulls me down into the crook of his arm, and kisses the top of my head. "Are you okay with this?"

"Yes. Are you?"

"Of course."

He drags his hand down my bare back and I bury my face in his chest trying to cope with the intensity of these sensations. He feels incredible, but the way he's acting makes it all so much more real. What does this mean? Where is this going? Are we doing it or not?

I can't stand waiting any longer. I rise on my elbow and start kissing him. He doesn't stop me and he doesn't try to slow things down when I stroke his chest, down his stomach, to his rock-hard package.

He groans when I start squeezing him and his fingertips close on my breast. I pant and whimper when he teases me. I need him so bad.

I'll go out of my mind if I wait any longer for him to make the first move. I ease my body on top of him and he responds with the same slow, deliberate relaxed air. He caresses down my sides, cups my cheeks to kiss me, and plays with my breasts until I can't stand it another second. I have to have him.

I sit up and take hold of his belt. He doesn't stop me and he doesn't stop gazing into my eyes while I unbuckle it and unzip his fly. He stretches out on the bed and raises his chiseled arms over his head while I slide his pants off.

I kick my jeans away and climb on top of him. Is he ever going to do anything or he just going to lie there and let me have my way with him?

I don't care anymore. I kiss him as hungrily as I want to and straddle him, but just as I'm getting ready to sit down on him, he rears off the bed with unbelievable power.

He grabs me and flips me over onto my back. He rises above me swelling so big that I catch my breath. He looks beastly and mesmerizing and unstoppable like this.

He attacks my mouth, and before I can think twice, he slides between my legs. Isn't this what I wanted? Isn't this what I was just planning to do?

His sudden move takes me by surprise, but it's the commanding glint in his eye that holds me captive. He drives in all the way to the hilt, and when he pulls away from my mouth to lock onto my eyes, he holds me there in an unbreakable grip.

"I'm gonna put my baby in you," he growls. "I'm gonna plant my seed in you and make you grow my baby. Is that what you want? Do you want my baby in there?"

I can barely whisper, "Yes!" His unbreakable gaze buckles my will to resist and that first powerful thrust explodes me in half.

I scream and contort on his masterful rhythm.

"You want that, baby?" he asks more loudly so he can make himself heard over my screams. "Is that what you want? Huh? Do you want me to put my baby in you? Huh? You want to carry my baby, don't you?"

Those words cast a spell over my mind. He's doing it. He's turning my body into the vehicle that will carry his baby. His baby. He's taking over. He's claiming this baby as his and bending my will to become his.....

Is this real? Is he saying he wants it to be real?

The baby is real. I'm already carrying it, but these deep, hard, slow, intense thrusts change everything I thought I knew about carrying a baby—his baby. He wants to plant his seed in me and make this HIS baby.

I can't stop this feeling of wanting him to do it. I want him to plant that seed and make me grow like this. I want this to be his baby as well as mine. I don't want to do this all by myself.

I try to hide in his chest from the waves of brutal pleasure sweeping over me. "Look at me, baby!" he commands and I have to look up into his hypnotic green eyes. When did those eyes become so powerful and intense?

He arches down and kisses me on the next stroke. I scream and cry into his mouth, but he won't let me get away. I don't want to. I want to feel him claiming my body as the fertile soil where he'll plant his essence. This is all becoming too, too real too fast.

He grunts and groans with rising pleasure. His body feels unbreakably hard and strong and true. I can't stop touching him, but my touch doesn't affect his rhythm. My screams only encourage him to work deeper, slower, more perfectly.

"Mine!" he snarls. "My baby! This is mine. Understand?"

I can only scream as catastrophic explosions burst in my brain. I can't hold on any longer. I arch into his thrusts and my legs crack apart to let him in. God, I want him in there! I want his baby in there. I want a piece of him living in me.

It spreads his vital essence through me until it consumes every particle of my being. It rewrites the nature of my cells and makes me the soil that will grow his baby for him.

He tears off my mouth, gasps once in brutal satisfaction, and dives into my neck. He leaves hot, biting kisses down my neck, rears up to catch my drunken eyes, and then dives for my chest.

He steals one torturous kiss after another in between rising up to make sure I'm still where he wants me. His titanic body expands with masculine power. How did a man ever get this big, this masterful, this supreme?

I can't take this. I keep screaming every time he says, "My baby!" Those words rocket through me and tear me to pieces with their power and meaning. They change everything, including me.

I need everything he is and everything he's doing to me. I can't do this alone. I need him to own this and make this baby his. I never realized how much I needed this.

I keep screaming as one explosive climax after another takes me out of this world. His body electrifies me so much that I barely notice when he picks up speed and finally plunges in hard.

His hot seed floods me....and it's finished. The deed is done. I'm carrying his baby and now nothing can ever be the same. How did this happen?

He did this. He must know so much more about all of this than I do. How did I ever think he was lifeless and bloodless and heartless?

He eases off and starts kissing me. His body keeps gliding on this river of bliss that floods my whole being with rapture. He's doing this, too. He's taking me somewhere.....Is this the Mountain of Mystery? Is he one of the people who will show me the way and help me overcome the obstacles?

I whimper in an agony of completion feeling the last tremors of delight wash out of my body. He pulls off my mouth with a deep, delicious smack, but he isn't finished yet. He migrates down my neck and starts kissing and sucking my nipples.

He massages my breasts so magically that I don't want to think about what this means. Is he celebrating me becoming a mother?

I can't deny it anymore when he inches down my stomach, rests his head right below my navel, and kisses me just above my pubic bone. He nuzzles in close to my skin, breathes on me, and I hear him whispering into my stomach.

That sound brings tears to my eyes and I hug his head close to me. I don't want this to end. I don't want to break the spell, but I know I have to. I have to leave to go back to my car and my own apartment. I have a job and a company to run. I have a life that doesn't include Damian.

He wraps his arms around my hips and buries his face in my stomach. So much emotion floods me that I can't cope with it. What is this? Why is this so hard and so important?

He finally rests his ear against my stomach and lets out a long, heartfelt sigh of happiness. He doesn't let me go. I only wish he felt this way about me instead of the baby—as well as the baby—but that's never going to happen.

Chapter 10: Damian

I thread my fingers together behind my head while I watch Juliet get dressed. I don't want her to leave, but she obviously doesn't want to stay.

I don't know what's happening to me. This baby business is changing everything I thought I knew about my life.

This baby is coming to mean way more to me than I ever thought it would. I want to be a father—the right kind of father —but I want something more than that. I want her. I want her and the baby in my life—the right way.

That's never going to happen, though. She might like having sex with me, but she'll never share her life with me. She's made that clear way too many times and now she's pulling on her jeans and putting on her bra to leave.

She sits on the edge of the bed with her back to me. She pretends not to notice me lying here relaxed and happy that I just did it with her. I want her to cuddle up with me and spend the rest of Saturday afternoon fooling around in my bed, but she doesn't look at me.

She surprises me by speaking over her shoulder, "Can I ask you a question?"

"Sure. Go ahead."

"You know the end sequence of the film where Little Boy Jake takes the rainbow treasure chest back to his family?"

"Yeah? What about it?"

"Do you think it's all right? Do you think I should change the family somehow?"

"I never thought about it. Why do you ask? What do you think is wrong with it?"

"I don't know." She bends down and starts tying her shoes. "I've never collaborated on anything like this before. Maybe it's just because we're working on it together that makes me question whether it's right. I thought you might have some idea on how to improve it."

"Is that what we're doing—collaborating?"

She turns around and smiles at me, and now that I see her eyes, I can't deny that she feels.....something. I don't know what, but she isn't as indifferent to me as I thought.

"You're making changes to the sequence and I'm incorporating them," she tells me. "I'm asking for your input on how we should make it better. We're collaborating."

"I've never collaborated on anything like this before, either. In fact, I've never done any animation at all. You're the expert."

"You shouldn't doubt yourself. You're really good."

"I'm glad you think so."

She beams at me even more broadly and quickly squeezes my lower leg. "I gotta go get my car and go home. Could you....you know...." She shoots a smirk at my body. "Get your clothes on.....or were you planning to drive me across town like that?"

I laugh and start to get up. I wasn't procrastinating because I planned to drive her across town like this. I just want to postpone the inevitable moment when she leaves my apartment.

Claiming this baby as mine somehow made her mine, too. I just don't know how that will work considering how independent she is—how independent both of us are.

I don't know what I'm thinking. She isn't mine and I don't even know if I want her to be. I wouldn't want her to be if she doesn't want to be and she obviously doesn't.

She leaves the bedroom while I get dressed, and when I go downstairs, I find her in the dining room bending over my drawings and laughing. "Are you sure you don't want to quit your job and come be a penniless animator with Ian and Frank?"

"You aren't penniless," I tell her. "I've seen your balance sheet, remember?"

She turns away and lets her hair fall over her face so I can't see her expression. What is she thinking?

I go over to her and pull her up to face me. I drown in those eyes for what seems like a long time. "I really enjoyed today."

Her cheeks color and she tries to look away, but I cradle her cheeks in both hands make her look at me while I kiss her. I really don't want her to leave. Doing it with her this time means something. It almost hurts to think of her leaving.

"Are we.....are we going to keep doing this?" she asks.

"If you want to. I would love it if you decided to come over again."

"I mean....." She trails off and doesn't finish.

I don't want to think about what it means. How would it work if we raised a kid separately and kept fooling around on the side? How would that affect a kid if his or her single parents were doing it behind closed doors?

She breaks eye contact and glances down at the pictures. "Do you think you'll do anything with these?"

"Do anything—like what?" I ask.

"I don't know. You could turn them into animated sequences or comics or children's books. You could do just about anything with them."

My eyes fly open. "You can't be serious."

"Sure, I am. Why not?"

"Naw!" I counter. "I couldn't do anything like that. This was just for fun—just to see if I still could."

"You should think about it. You're really good—good enough to be a professional."

She looks back down at them and they pull her attention away from me. Is she only interested in me for this? Her whole attitude changed toward me when she saw my drawings.

I don't want her here if she's more interested in my drawings than she is in me. I turn away. "Come on. I'll drive you back to your car."

I kiss her again before I let her out of the car. She drives off and I go back to my apartment. I get some work done in my home office, but I keep wandering into the dining room to add to and adjust the sketches I've already done and to make new ones as they pop into my head.

I'm not sure where this is all going, but things come to a tipping point when I get to work on Monday morning.

I go to my office and start going through my dailies and preparing my schedule. I check the designers' progress on all our ongoing jobs and my stomach turns when I see their art. Why am I only noticing now how stilted and lifeless they are?

All the people in all the images look like Squares....because they are Squares. Jesus Christ, what have I created?

I flip through every job and see the same thing everywhere. I never had a problem letting my artists do their thing. Their work always looked fine to me before. It looked more than fine. It looked outstanding.

Now I see everything wrong with it. I see the way I would draw it if I was the artist handling these projects. I can't stand to look at them.

I go downstairs to the design studio and go into my design manager Phoebe McCleod's office. "What's up?" she asks me. "To what do we owe the pleasure of a visit from On High?"

I pull out my tablet and lay it on her desk. I swipe to the first few images and sketch on them with my pen.

"Don't you think this would look better with more definition in the cloud pattern here? And I think you should add more expression to the face on this one. It looks bland and the eyes make the character look indifferent. This one is too dark. Look what happens when I lighten the background.....and you could add a few highlights to the person's face so it looks like they're looking up into the light. This one needs to be longer—it's too short—and make these houses shorter and wider and curve the walls outward so they look fat. Add some movement lines here and here so it looks like the houses are moving and jumping around on the grass.....See?"

She blinks down at my tablet and then up at me. "Uh....okay."

"Do you have a problem with any of that? Do you think anything's wrong with it?"

"Of course not. You're the boss. If you say it should be that way, then...."

"I'm asking for your creative input. If you think there's anything wrong with this, tell me now."

"No, I don't think there's anything wrong with it. It's just...." She narrows her eyes at me. "Why are you doing this? You've never stuck your nose in our designs before."

"Is that what I'm doing—sticking my nose in?"

"That's not what I mean. This is just so.....creative."

I burst out laughing and pick up my tablet. "I'm emailing you the changes. I have a few more projects to go over and I'll send you any changes to them, too."

"So....is this going to become a regular thing—you getting involved in the creative side of this company?"

"Probably. I don't know. I guess it depends if I see anything that needs me to get involved."

She grins at me. "You could become a graphic designer and move out of that fancy office upstairs. You could come down here and slum it with us."

I laugh and go back upstairs. I'm already a graphic designer. I've been a graphic designer since high school. That's how I built this company, but I don't tell her that. Something weird is happening to me.

I go back to my office and scroll through the rest of the projects on our roster. Some are far enough along in the production process that it's too late to change the art. I cringe when I see it. I can see now how much better it could have been.

I bombard Phoebe with emails all day long including sketches, pictures, and alterations to the images the designers have already produced, but when she sends me back the completed designs, they look lightyears better. I should have been doing this all along instead of leaving design to someone else.

I get a few more ideas for the drawings I'm doing at home, but when I rummage in my desk, I can't find a notebook or even any scratch paper. Is it possible that I've been living all these years without even a pencil or a piece of paper to doodle on? That has to change.

I go out on my lunch break and hit the stores, but when I get into the notebook aisle, I spend way too much time checking out all the art supplies. The horse has definitely left the barn on my creative energies.

I wind up buying a much bigger art sketchbook and another set of colored pencils just for the office. I don't want to miss out on my next great idea just because I didn't have the supplies on hand.

I set up the sketchbook and pencils on the side of my desk next to my computer. I find myself turning aside and doodling, sketching, and shading while I think about business, talk on the phone, or in between projects when I need to make any kind of decision.

Doing it this way doesn't distract me as much as I thought it would. It doesn't distract me at all. It actually helps me concentrate and I end up getting more done than ever before.

I feel happier than I've ever felt at work before. I always just took care of business. I never got any joy out of it before. What was I thinking letting this slip out of my life?

Halfway through the afternoon, a new project proposal comes through from one of our long-term clients. It's from the local Hummingridge Mall that always caters to higher-end clientele.

They want to do a marketing campaign targeting kids and high-end parents who want to shop for their kids. The mall directors are installing a lower level with a big jungle gym, trampoline park, climbing wall, and play area adjacent to the food court. They want to pitch it as a place where kids can hang out and play while their parents eat, shop, and hang out.

The mall directors send me over a few pictures of the play area design. They want to incorporate the play area layout into the marketing campaign to show kids playing around and having fun there.

My mind blows with all the possibilities I've never thought of before. I start sketching on my pad, but I only get into the second drawing when I realize that I'm only mimicking designs I've already seen at Animatrix.

The penny drops and I realize. Animatrix's fun, childlike attitude would be perfect for this. I can just imagine what Juliet and her team of oversized kids would come up for this.

I pick up my phone to call Juliet when an email notification pops up on my computer. It's from Rex Atkins, the head of Masters Marketing's corporate legal team. He and his posse of sharks have been researching Animatrix in preparation for Masters Marketing to acquire the company.

I click open the email and find a bunch of screenshots attached to it. The first several are from Animatrix's website showing the list of major investors. The newest entries are for Paper Tiger Film Studios. They've just been added in the twenty-four hours.

The next batch of screenshots are of Animatrix's stockholder roster. The first one is from nine o'clock this morning—right before the market open. The second is from one hour ago and my stomach drops when I see Juliet Holloway's name right at the top.

She's just purchased an additional three thousand shares in her own company which pushes her total up to fifty-four percent of the company's public offering.

My energy drains away when I realize the terrible truth. She's gotten the funding to purchase a controlling share of her own company. Masters Marketing doesn't have a hope of acquiring Animatrix now.

Chapter 11: Juliet

I flip through Animatrix's schedule and beam at Ian sitting in the chair across from me. "Good job, buddy. You're on schedule with all your projects. I knew you could do it."

He kicks back in his seat, hooks his thumbs in his pockets, and smiles back at me. "You know, I feel better staying on schedule. I didn't realize how much falling behind was stressing me out. I feel a lot more relaxed and proud of my work, now that everything is on time."

"Great! That's wonderful. How would you like to take on some new projects?"

He spreads his arms. "Hit me, baby. I can accomplish anything."

I laugh and turn back to the schedule. "We just got a bunch of new jobs from Albertson's Pharmacy, Watson Foods, and one from Bridge Street School. Why don't you take the school job, and if you're feeling powerful, you can do the Watson Foods project, too."

"I'm feeling powerful now. I'm ready to take on the world."

"Let's test out your new superpowers before we send you into battle against Ultron for the fate of the multiverse."

"Aw, man!" He grins and gets to his feet. "When are you gonna introduce me to Ironman and the rest of the Avengers team?"

I can't help but grin at him while I walk him out of my office. "Knock this Bridge Street School job out of the park and I'll take you with me on my next date with Tony Stark."

He points at me and shakes his finger. "I knew you were dating him on the side! You're gonna be the next Lois Lane if you don't watch out."

"That's Superman, pal." I clap him on the shoulder. "Go on. Show me your mutant ninja animation abilities and we'll take it from there."

He extends his fist in front of him, cocks one knee, and zooms away making a swishing sound effect with his mouth. I turn back to my desk, and a second later, I hear Frank bellowing at Ian to pick up something he knocked over when he ran into it.

I chuckle on my way back to my desk. Life is beautiful, now that I've secured funding from Paper Tiger Film Studios to purchase a controlling share in Animatrix. I never have to worry ever again about Masters Marketing or anyone else taking Animatrix from me.

Now we have a bunch of new work and Animatrix is thriving more than ever. I'm feeling pretty good when I get an email notification from Bart Everette, one of the executive producers from Paper Tiger Film Studios.

My blood runs cold when I see the name on the email. Paper Tiger better not be thinking twice about investing in Animatrix. This purchase means too much to me and I don't know who I'd approach next if Paper Tiger backs out.

Bart asks to have a zoom meeting with me right away, which makes me even more nervous. What went wrong? What's the problem with Paper Tiger's investment? I don't want to find out, but I can't ignore a meeting request from my biggest investor.

I switch onto the call and Bart smiles at me from the screen. Is he smiling in a friendly way or because he's about to drop the ax on my neck?

"How's it going, Bart?" I ask and pray to Almighty God that I'm keeping my voice steady. "Is everything all right with the investment?"

"Forget the investment!" he blurts out. "I want to talk to you about something way more important."

"What's that?" What could be more important than Paper Tiger's investment?

He turns to the computer on the side of his desk. "I want to talk to you about that project schedule you sent through.....the one with your current projects that you let us take a look at to get us to invest in your company."

"Yeah?" I ask. "Is anything wrong with the schedule?"

"Not at all! We want to talk to you about a project the schedule says you're working on—the film about Little Boy Jake's quest to the Mountain of Mystery."

"Uh...okay. What about it?"

"We want to buy it. We want you to expand it into a complete feature and sell it to us so we can produce it for the wider market. It's hilarious....and timely. We love the message and the characters are perfect! The Squares are the best!"

"Yeah..." I mutter. "They're great."

"So what do you say? We could send you over a contract offering a very competitive sale price and you can have your legal team look it over. We'd love to have you and your negotiators meet us in the studio so we can hash this whole thing out."

"Um....." I stammer. "I'm collaborating on that one, so I would have to discuss that will my fellow artists....."

"Really?" He frowns at the schedule. "Your name is the only one on it."

"I know. My collaborator is working anonymous. I shouldn't have included the film in the schedule. It must have slipped by me."

"Well, let your collaborator know and I'll get our team to put together the contract for it. Then you can share it with your collaborator and you can bring her along when you come for the negotiation."

"Uh...okay, Bart. You do that and I'll talk to my collaborator."

We hang up and I sit there staring at the screen for a long time. Paper Tiger Film Studios wants to buy the Little Boy Jake film. Damian and I haven't even finished it.

Selling it would mean we would have to work together on it a lot more, but that doesn't concern me. Things have been going so well between us that I'm sure we could finish the film together.

I don't want to sell it, though. I created this film for our unborn child and this film is the reason Damian and I are getting along now. I hated him before this. I don't want to lose that....and I don't want to share it with anyone else, either.

This is between me and him....and our child. I want to keep it that way. I'm not sure I want anyone else in the world to see it. I wouldn't have sent it to Paper Tiger in the first place if I thought about it beforehand. I don't like that strangers have seen it.

I can think of a lot of other things I want to share with him and no one else—starting with this child.

I realize with a jolt that I want him to go to my doctor's appointments and ultrasounds and everything. I want to share those moments with him. Why wouldn't I? He's my baby's father. Damian is the one person in the world that will be there for all this child's milestones. This child and everything about it will always be just between him and me.

I want Damian to be there when the baby is born....and for everything else. Every moment of this child's life will be a milestone—a precious moment in time never to be repeated. How is one moment more important than any other?

Why wouldn't I want to share all those moments with Damian? Why wouldn't I want to look across the room at him and know that he knows and shares all those moments with me? Why would I want it to be otherwise? I wouldn't.

I pick up my phone and stare at the screen. Should I tell him? I have to tell him about Paper Tiger's offer. I couldn't keep this to myself.

I would have the legal right to block the sale even if he wants to sell the film, but I still have to tell him. Keeping it to myself would be wrong.....just like keeping this child to myself would be wrong.

I send him a text. We exchanged numbers when he dropped me off at my car on Saturday. He said he was doing it so I could let him know if anything happened with the pregnancy, but now the fact that I have his number means something so much more.

It almost feels like we're dating....or maybe that we've gone even past that. Are we a couple? We might as well be if we're having a child together. Are we really going to raise this child separately? That wouldn't be the right thing for the child, would it?

It wouldn't be the best thing for us, either. Seeing him across the room and knowing that he shares all those moments with me—that would be the best thing for me, too.

What about him? He was the one who said having a kid would destroy his life, but he's definitely changed his tune lately.

I tap out the message. *Howdy. Would you like to have dinner on Saturday night? Send.*

He replies right away. *I'd love to. Do you want to go back to the Oak Street Kitchen? I still haven't eaten anything there.*

I have to laugh reading his message. He really is funny. Why did I think he was wooden and humorless?

I haven't eaten anything there, either. Maybe we can become known as that creepy couple that comes in, never orders anything, and then leaves.

Is that what we're going to do? he asks. *Are we going to leave without eating anything?*

The blood rushes to my cheeks. No one has to paint me a picture of what he means. He's asking if we're going to leave the Oak Street Kitchen to go hook up. He's asking if that's the reason we'll never order any food.

How about we make a deal that we don't leave the café until we've both finished eating?

Deal, he replies. *Eight o'clock?*

Perfect.

I burst out laughing when he answers by sending me an emoji of a hot dog and then another one of a milkshake with a straw sticking out of the cup. I don't think the Oak Street Kitchen even serves hot dogs and milkshakes, but that doesn't matter.

He makes me laugh. My heart skips a beat when I scroll through the emojis on my phone and send him back one of a giraffe and another of a birthday cake.

I practically fall out of my chair when he sends me back one of a brain followed by one of a pair of lungs with the windpipe attached.

I'm still wiping tears of laughter out of my eyes when he sends one last text. *I gotta get back to work. Save the emojis for the weekend.* He follows this with a kiss emoji.

My heart turns another somersault looking at that kiss. Does that mean he wants us to be a couple? Is he thinking about sharing all those moments with me, too?

I guess I'll find out on Saturday.

Chapter 12: Damian

I fight down nerves when I get to the Oak Street Kitchen ten minutes early. I don't want to take the chance that Juliet will get here before me. I tell the hostess which table I want. Another couple is sitting there, but she tells me that they're almost done. I can wait five minutes.

I sit down facing the door and command myself not to fidget. I never expected Juliet to ask me out. Maybe I got it all wrong and she wants more, too.

I make a point of not freaking out when she finally walks in. She's wearing casual khaki pants and flat shoes—not what I would expect for a date—not that she asked me out on a date. She only asked me to have dinner with her, but that's a lot more than she's ever done before.

I stand up and go out to meet her. I restrain myself from hugging and kissing her until I know what she wants to do. I don't want to screw this up by presuming.

I also don't pull out her chair for her. She sits down and smiles at me. "How's it going?"

"Good," I tell her. "I was surprised that you asked me out."

She blushes. "Yeah, well, I had to. I got an offer from Paper Tiger Film Studios to buy the Little Boy Jake film. I had to check with you since we're collaborating."

My spirits wilt. Is that the only reason she asked me to have dinner—to talk business? I'm glad now that I didn't presume or try to make this into a date.

"I didn't want to assume anything in case you decided that you did want to sell it," she goes on. "You said you didn't want to do anything with your art, but maybe now that you have a solid offer, you want to rethink that. Paper Tiger isn't the biggest studio, but they always offer competitive compensation. Anything you produced for them could lead to something bigger."

"I....I don't know what to say," I stammer. "I wasn't expecting this."

"Neither was I. I sent them our project schedule as part of my pitch to secure their investment in Animatrix. I didn't even realize the film was on the schedule until their exec made the offer. I wouldn't have sent it if I knew it would come to this."

"Why not? Isn't the film good enough?"

"Of course it's good enough! They wouldn't offer if it wasn't and it's as good as it is because of you."

I shrug that off. "I don't know about that."

"Why do you keep doubting yourself? It's so much better with the changes you made....and he loved the Squares. The film is as much yours as mine. I could totally understand if you wanted to sell it."

I look away trying to think. "I don't know if I want to or not."

"Like I said, it might not do anything, but it would be a film credit for you in case you wanted to do something bigger and more ambitious—something under your own name. It's the first building block in a portfolio that other producers can see and use to judge your work."

I roll my eyes and groan. "I don't want anyone judging my work."

"You should consider it. You could be amazing. You could be the next Stan Lee."

I burst out laughing. "Stop it!"

She beams at me until I manage to get serious again. "It sounds like you really want to sell it. You should. You deserve it."

Her face drains of all color and her eyes go cold and....scared. "No. I don't."

"You don't? Why not? Why are you encouraging me to do it if you don't want to? Neither of us can sell it without the other's permission. If you don't want to sell it, why are you even telling me? You could tell your exec that it isn't for sale. Why are we even having this conversation?"

"I had to tell you. I couldn't leave you in the dark. Besides, I didn't want you to find out about the offer after the fact in case you did want to sell it. I had to at least give you the chance to consider it."

"So why don't you want to sell it?" I ask. "You just said it's good enough."

She looks away before she finally manages to meet my gaze. "I just want....I want the film to be just between us. It's the one good thing that's happened between us....I mean apart from having a child together. We have this child in common, but the film is what brought us together. I don't want to share that with anyone. I wouldn't have let anyone see it if I had thought of it before. I wish now that no one had ever seen it. I want it be just between us....the three of us.....almost like....." She falters and looks down at her hands on the table. She won't look at me when she chokes out the next words. "Almost like we're a family."

Those words stab me in the heart and I don't try to stop myself from covering her hands with mine. Family. Are we going to be a family? Is that what we are?

We would have to be if we're this child's parents. I can't believe she just said those words. She doesn't want to share the film with anyone but me.

She's right. Having a child together didn't bring us together. The film did that. We're having this conversation and I'm touching her hand right now because of the film. She hated me before we started working on this.

She still won't look at me when she turns her hand over and squeezes mine. Without even trying, we both thread our fingers together and grip each other tight. Does this mean what I think it means? Are we really going there?

She keeps her eyes down and I can't read her expression. She looks sad and scared and angry all at the same time.

"Look at me, baby," I whisper.

Her eyes shoot up and her expression changes when our gazes lock. She's indescribably beautiful like this—so open and vulnerable and uncertain. She's a thousand times more beautiful right now than she was on the *Dream Dimension* or in my room or anywhere else I've seen her.

I can't believe I'm looking at the same woman. I hardly recognize her. She looks so beautiful that I don't know if I can stand the emotion welling up in my heart right now.

I crush her hand and gulp down the urge to kiss her. Her eyes skip sideways at some of the other diners. "So.....neither of us can leave until we finish eating...right?"

I burst out laughing again. I don't know why. Maybe it's because I'm so fucking happy to be sitting here with her. I don't care if this turns into something more. We're having this kid together and I'm sitting here holding her hand.

"We better order then," I tell her and pick up her hand. I give her a quick kiss on the knuckles and pull the menus out from behind the napkin dispenser.

I hand her one menu and open mine, but it takes a lot for me to concentrate on it. I just want to keep looking at her forever.

She studies her menu for half a second and puts it back. "What are you getting?" I ask. "Are you going to order one French fry so you could get out of here faster?"

Now it's her turn to laugh and she blushes. "Why would I want to get out of here faster?"

I find my cheeks burning when I laugh. She always knows how to lighten the mood even when she's dropping a suggestion like that. Why would she want to get out of here faster if she isn't going to come back to my place?

What would happen if I took her back to my place? Would we spend all night together? Would we talk about art.....or would we spend the whole time cracking jokes?

I can't decide which would be better. I would be happy to spend all night doing any of those things with her. I can't think of anything I'd rather do.

She smirks at my menu. "Do you need help? Would you like me to order for you?"

"I think you better. I'm not getting anything done over here." I hand her the menu. "Just order me something more than French fries."

She blushes and grins over the menu. "Do you have any dietary requirements?"

"I'm allergic to bullshit."

She explodes with laughter and puts the menu away. "They definitely don't serve that here."

"What are you getting me?"

"You'll just have to wait and find out. You're leaving me in charge, so you don't get to make decisions for yourself."

I can't take my eyes off her, and as soon as she finishes mouthing off to me, I slide my hand across the table and take hers again.

She doesn't have any trouble smiling at me now and we stay there holding hands until the waiter comes. The guy flips his notepad to a new page and his pen hangs suspended over the paper. "What can I get for you tonight?"

"I'll have the fried calamari platter," she tells him, "and he'll have the shrimp jambalaya....and for drinks, I'll have a glass of chardonnay and he'll have a gin and tonic."

"Thank you," the guy replies and takes off for the kitchen.

"How did you know I like gin and tonics?" I ask.

"You were drinking one when I saw you at the bar on the *Dream Dimension*."

I shake my head. "Your memory is better than mine. I don't remember what you were drinking."

"Let's just say you made an impression."

"Not a very good one, apparently. You said I was the last person you would ever want to invest in your business."

She colors and looks away. "I said a lot of things to you that I shouldn't have. I regret that now."

"You were right. I was bloodless and lifeless and heartless. This film gave me that back. *You* gave me that back."

Her eyes soften and she strokes her thumb across the back of my hand. "I can't take credit for your creativity. That's all you."

"So....and I still a Square?" I ask.

She bursts out laughing. "Well, you do still wear a suit."

I love talking to her. She makes it so easy.

"So what are you working on now?" she asks. "Have you started on your apartment walls yet?"

"Not yet, but I'm thinking about starting something."

"What?" she asks.

"I don't know. I've been drawing non-stop since last weekend. I have to do something with all this stuff that keeps coming out of my head."

"I guess you had however many years of ideas lying dormant under the surface. You tapped the well and now it's overflowing."

"I hope you're right. I'm going to need a bigger apartment if this keeps up."

She laughs and her eyes gleam with some buried message. I have to look deep, deep into her to figure it out and I still don't understand what it is she's trying to tell me.

"So what will you do with it?" she asks.

"I don't know. I guess I keep thinking about your suggestions—about doing animation or a comic or maybe a children's book. There has to be some outlet for all this. I don't know why I thought I could get through the rest of my life without expressing....whatever it is I'm trying to express."

She beams at me across the table. Her eyes shine with so much mesmerizing energy that I don't know what to think.

Neither of us says anything for a minute, and just then, the waiter comes back with our drinks. We both sip our drinks, and just when I'm starting to wonder what to say to restart the conversation, he comes back with our food.

"Thank you for this," I tell her when I pull my plate toward me. "I love seafood."

"I guessed when I saw the way you were moving around on the *Dream Dimension*."

"You mean falling all over myself and nearly getting drowned?"

"No, before that. You were walking around the boat like you'd been out at sea before. Then, just now when you opened the menu, you flipped straight past the meat and vegetarian sections and went straight to the seafood section."

"You're a better detective than I am. I never would have pegged you for a calamari girl."

"You should have. I only ordered this for the comic value." She picks up two curly snarls of calamari. They've been deep-fried into two matched bouquets of tentacles twisted in all kinds of crazy shapes.

She rotates them up and down in her fingertips and starts singing a silly song to match their movements. She makes them dance around so they look like otherworldly cartoon characters.

I burst out laughing and almost choke on my drink. "Let me guess. You ordered *this* for the comic value, too." I spike a shrimp on my fork and raise it in the air between us. I undulate it back and forth so it looks like it's swimming through the air. I come up with a bee-bopping tune on the fly and add a few bubbling sounds to go with it.

She dissolves in laughter and nearly falls out of her chair when I position all the shrimp on my plate in a line with their tentacles pointed in the same direction. I arrange them in a long single-file queue marching over the top of my pile of rice.

"It's the Great Pacific Migration. We're on your way to the Great Barrier Reef for our annual mating season." I jump out of my seat, point at her, and practically yell for the whole restaurant to hear. "Oh! I got it! We can add another species to the Mountain of Mystery quest! It's the Shrimptapus....No, the Prawnigators!"

She's laughing too hard to speak and tears pour down her cheeks as she hugs her ribs. I raise my forked shrimps and move them around in a way that makes their feelers wobble.

"They're swimming through the Brundle Sea all going the same direction," I narrate. "They don't know what danger lies ahead, but they have to keep going in the same direction because the Shrimptapus in front of them are going that way. They never think for themselves."

"Stop!!" she croaks. "You're killing me!"

I put my shrimps down chuckling. I love making her laugh. "I'm definitely adding the Shrimptapus to the film. Just letting you know."

She laughs a few more times and wipes her eyes on her napkin. "You said you were calling them Prawnigators," and she breaks down laughing again.

"I'll come up with a better name." I start eating, but it takes Juliet a few more minutes before she composes herself enough to put her food in her mouth.

"Don't say anything else until we finish eating, okay?" she tells me. "I don't think I can take it."

"I can make you laugh without saying anything." I spike another shrimp, swim it through the air, open my mouth really wide, and make deep, monstrous groaning noises like I'm a monster about to swallow the shrimp.

Then, when it gets close enough, I start making screaming noises and jiggle the shrimp around like it's struggling to escape.

Juliet dissolves in laughter again and people at nearby tables turn to watch. A few of them start laughing, too, so I must be doing something right.

I finally wrestle the shrimp into my mouth and drop the act while I chew it up. Juliet really has to fight herself under control and I don't pull any other silly antics when she starts eating. I could make her spit her food all over the table, but I'm enjoying this too much.

I can't help studying her while we eat and I don't say anything else. She wakes something in me that I never knew was there. I never thought of myself as funny or comical or silly. I've never made anyone laugh this much in my life.

She makes me want to fool around and be stupid and childish. She makes me want to have fun and I want her to have fun when she's with me. I want her to love every minute with me. I want her to love every minute as much as I love every minute with her.

Am I really thinking that? I get the thrill of my life when she grins and snickers during dinner. What's going to happen when we finally finish eating and it's time to leave?

We get through the rest of the meal and our drinks without busting a gut. I love gazing at her and her eyes sparkle when she smiles at me. Is she thinking what I'm thinking?

We finally leave and I walk her out to the parking lot. "So....are you really going to add those shrimp to the film?" she asks.

"Shrimptapus," I correct. "Please. Call them by the correct taxonomical name for the purpose of scientific identification."

She laughs, and now that we're outside, I can finally move close to her. I slip my hand into hers and pull her close to me.

She gets serious real faster and her eyes tell me all I need to know. "So....are we.....you know.....?"

I cradle her cheeks in both hands. "I'd love to, but I think we should save that for next time."

"Is there going to be a next time?"

"I'd like there to be. I'd like it to be all the time."

Her eyes widen. "You would?"

"Of course I would. Do you really have to ask?" I kiss her and let my lips linger extra slow on her delicious mouth. "I want everything."

Her breath catches and her eyes don't leave my face, so I guess that's a good reaction.

I indulge in a long, deep kiss and she gulps when I ease back and look into her eyes. "Maybe next time, I could pick you up and drive you....." I suggest, "like a real date. Would you like that?"

She nods and gulps again. Good. "Next Saturday?" I ask. "Eight o'clock?"

"Uh...okay...." She can barely speak above a whisper.

I ease in and kiss her one more time....long.....slow.....deep. She's beyond perfect. I love kissing her like this. Not taking her home is almost better than taking her home. I'm going to see her next Saturday. I can wait and make the investment in something even better if it's going to last.

Chapter 13: Juliet

I come out of my office and try not to look at anyone on my way to the front of the main floor. "Hey, Juliet!" Sophie calls from behind me. "Did you see the dancing tomatoes that Ian came up with for the Watson Foods ad? They're the best!"

"I'll see them when I check the project schedule this afternoon. I have a client meeting right now."

"Who with?" Frank asks.

I keep my head turned so no one will see me blushing. "It's with Masters Marketing."

A chill falls over the room. "You mean the same assholes that tried to buy us out?" Ian asks.

"They aren't here to buy us out. They're here as clients so make sure you freaks behave yourselves."

Ian grabs his pen holder, tips it over, and puts a bunch of pens in his mouth. They dangle from his lips and stick down toward his chin like giant fangs. He makes grunting noises and Frank joins in.

He grabs a suction-cup dancing flower pot off the top of his monitor, stabs the suction cup onto his forehead with a loud smack, and starts rushing Ian. Frank bows his head like he wants to spike Ian with the flower. It wobbles and waves around in ridiculous spirals.

Ian makes his noises louder and Frank starts making high-pitched neighing sounds while he tries to impale Ian with his flower.

The whole floor explodes in laughter and I have to join in until, without warning, dead quiet falls over the staff. People stare at me in horror and then jump back into their seats.

Frank and Ian keep going for a second, but everyone else is acting so strangely and I can't figure out why until the door shuts behind me.

I spin around to see Damian standing there watching the last of the mayhem taking place in my office.

Frank and Ian realize an instant later and they stop horsing around. They both slink back to their computers, put their stuff back in its proper place, and pretend to go back to work.

"Sorry," I tell Damian. "I'm sorry you had to see that."

"It's okay. You guys have a culture that works for you and I'm glad your staff can have fun at work. That's important, especially in your business."

I change the subject by waving to one side. "Shall we get started? Follow me. I'll show you where we can talk without being disturbed."

Every eye in the room follows me and Damian to the meeting room adjacent to the main floor. None of these people know about me being pregnant yet. To them, Damian is the Devil Incarnate who tried to buy out Animatrix.

I'm going to have to break the news sooner or later. I wouldn't be so concerned about my staff finding out that I'm going to have a kid. This child is probably going to be spending a lot of time in the office. I can just imagine what kind of influence my animators are going to be on this child.

I laugh thinking about this child joining in the goofy antics around the office and Damian spins around to stare at me. "What's so funny?"

"Nothing. Nothing at all. Come on in."

I open the door to the meeting room and try to put on my best big-bad-boss mask. This is a business meeting and Damian is a client. I need to treat this meeting with the seriousness it deserves, but all my experiences with him don't make it easy.

He's been making me laugh nonstop since this whole thing started and the drawings he sent me for the Shrimpticles are beyond anything he's come up with so far. He changed the name after he went home and I'm still stunned that he can come up with so much material so fast. He must be drawing all the time now. He definitely let the genie out of the bottle and there's no putting it back.

I motion to a chair across the table from me. "Take a seat. I got the material you sent over for the Hummingridge Mall campaign and I think you're onto something great with your animation concept."

"I came up with another few ideas after I sent it." He unzips his black nylon folder. I start to eye the folder like it's Pandora's box about to disgorge another torrent of creative madness on the world.

He rotates the folder toward me so I can see his drawings. He's done them all in the same colored pencils. "Your work is developing by leaps and bounds!" I tell him. "I can tell you've refined your style even in the last couple of weeks."

"You think so? I can definitely see room for improvement."

I laugh as I turn over the sheets in front of me. "These are really cool! I love where you're going with this."

"Don't just take my ideas and animate them," he tells me. "I'm hiring you to add Animatrix's unique flavor to this project. I want you to take these and run with them. Change them around and add to them so you bring them to life the way you always do. Put your stamp on them."

"Oh, I will!" I beam at him and then wake up my tablet. "I came up with a few ideas after you sent me your original concept material.

I think we should combine this slide idea of mine with your trampo-line sequence. We can have the child sliding down the slide, the slide twisting around and coming to life, shooting the kid into the air, and then they come down and bounce on a trampoline at the bottom with the movements you used in this image here...."

I pull up some of his previous drawings and add it in at the end of the slide sequence.

"Perfect!" He flips a few more sheets in the folder. "It would be great if we could somehow merge the trampoline sequence with this bubble concept from the mall directors."

"I was thinking the same thing." I swipe my tablet to another video player. "I came up with this bubble popping and the child inside falling into a set of clothes from one of the stores.....here."

I show him the sketches I used to combine some of the clothes photos the mall directors sent with my cartoon child falling into them. The little person winds up dressed in a thick winter skiing suit and the bouncy trampoline surface from the previous sequence transforms into a snowy ski slope that the child skis down.

Damian stares at it and then starts laughing. "This is great! This is exactly what I want."

"Do you want to keep sending me pictures as you come up with them or do you want us to take it from here?" I ask.

He blushes and pretends to look away. "I better not. I'm supposed to be the CEO of a major corporation. My graphic designers are al-ready having nervous breakdowns because I'm getting too involved in their projects."

I have to laugh. "Are you getting any real work done or is it all art now?"

"That's the weird thing. I get more done now than I did before. Drawing all day long seems to make me more productive. I should have been doing this years ago. I just didn't know I would react to it like I have."

Listening to him makes me want to kiss him. His face shines with happiness. He really looks delighted that he has his art back in his life.

"Anyway…." He tries to shrug it off. "I should keep out of it and let you run with it. You're the experts. I'm just a Square."

"No!" I tell him. "Not at all. You're really good. I would love it if you sent me whatever you think of."

"Really?" he asks. "You aren't just saying that?"

"Of course not. What you've come up with so far is great. I'm sure whatever you think of in the future will be just as useful. We'll incorporate it and make it even better."

"So….are we collaborating?"

I laugh again and find myself blushing. "Definitely."

He beams at me with that look glistening in his eyes. He lowers his voice to a confidential murmur. "I really want to kiss you right now."

"Maybe save that for next time."

"I'll save it for Saturday. Are we done here?"

"Until you send me some more drawings."

He laughs and his cheeks flush while he zips up his folder. "I'm glad you like them."

"I love them." I stop myself just in time from saying the next words that almost fall off the tip of my tongue. I'm not ready to say that yet.

He stands up and tucks his folder under his arm. "I'll get out of your hair now."

He moves over to the door and my heart flips. I don't want him to leave. I love hanging out with him and talking art and collaborating on everything. I just want it to keep going forever.

"Damian!" I call after him.

He turns back on the threshold. "Yeah?"

"I....uh.....I have a doctor's appointment on Friday.....if you want to come."

He bursts into a huge grin. "I'd love to. Text me the time and place and I'll be there."

My spirits deflate when he walks out and leaves me standing alone in the meeting room with his drawings. Now that he's gone, I wish I handled that last exchange differently.

I wish now that he was driving me to my doctor's appointment instead of us going separately like two strangers who got pregnant accidentally. I wish we were going....as a couple.

I can finally admit to myself that I want that. I want us to be a couple. I want that for the child and for myself. I want this to be real.

I want us to go to my doctor's appointments as a couple. I want us to share those moments knowing that we're laying the foundation of a future that will last a lifetime. I want my child to know that their parents were united in love and joy about this child's birth from the very beginning. I don't want this child ever to find out that we were strangers who hooked up unexpectedly.

Does Damian feel the same way? He sure acted that way on our date last Saturday. I wish I had the courage to just come right out and tell him that this is what I want. I wish I didn't have to keep up this armor of always being independent. Will I ever be able to let him in?

Thinking that scares the shit out of me. The idea of sharing my life with anyone scares me, but thinking about sharing it with him terrifies the pants off me. I shudder just thinking about it even as I ache for it. What is wrong with me? Why can't I just let myself be happy?

I want this child to be happy and that means being a couple with Damian. I have to do it for the child. As long as I think that, I can go through with it.

That isn't good enough, though. I need to be a couple with Damian for myself. I need to let him know that I.....that I.....

I can't think that. I can't think that I love him when we barely know each other. I hooked up with him a few times and we went out to dinner once. We haven't even had our first real date yet. I can't start thinking that way about him.

I'm thinking about it anyway. I can't stop thinking about it.

Chapter 14: Damian

I'm having serious heart palpitations standing outside the medical center waiting for Juliet to show up. I don't let myself pace up and down or I might have to admit that I'm really nervous. I'm beyond nervous. I'm a nervous wreck. If I'm this nervous about a doctor's appointment, how am I going to handle the baby's birth?

This is nothing. This is one doctor's appointment, but I still feel like my whole future hangs on this one appointment. What if something is wrong with Juliet? What if I find out that she has some really unhealthy habit that could put the baby in danger?

I know she doesn't, but my imagination runs away with me anyway. I keep coming up with horrific scenarios about something going wrong with the pregnancy. That would be my worst nightmare considering how invested I am in this now.

I have to fight myself not to grill Juliet about everything she eats, how much sleep she gets, what kind of body lotion she uses and whether it has any harmful chemicals in it, whether her apartment is too near the highway in case the air quality isn't good enough.....

I want to control everything she does, who she talks to, what she eats, what she watches, and even what she thinks. Everything she does affects my baby, but I can't do any of that without coming across as a creepy controlling asshole.

She has become intertwined with my baby so that I'm as concerned about her wellbeing as I am about the baby's. I want to make sure she only has the best, not just so the baby will be as healthy and thriving as possible, but so she will be, too. I care. That's the truth. I care as much about her as I do about the baby.

They're the same being to me now. I can't have one without the other and I don't want one without the other. I want it all. I want her to love......me. There. I thought those words.

I don't just want her to love me caring about her and the baby. I don't just want her to love hanging out with me and joking and sharing our art and our work lives. I don't just want her to love going out with me and collaborating on projects.

I want her to love me. I want her to want me and I want her to want to be with me as much as I want to be with her.

I just wish I could tell her. I wish I could come out and lay it all out on the table. I don't want her to be independent. That's the bottom line. I want her to need me. I want her to rely on me for something she can't get by herself. I want to be a crucial part of her life that she can't live without.

Is it wrong to think that? Is it wrong to want to make her less independent? I could never tell her that. She would just go back to hating me if I said that.

It would be better for us to live separately and raise this child separately than to risk letting her go back to hating me. I couldn't do that. I don't want that. I don't want her to be less independent. I love that she's independent.

Christ, what is wrong with me? I don't understand half the thoughts running through my head. I wish I did. I feel like I'm going out of my mind.

I practically collapse when she pulls into the parking lot. She smiles at me when she gets out of her car and walks over to me. "Hi."

"Hi," I reply. "Are you all good?"

She nods. She keeps looking around at nothing. Is she as nervous as I am?

"Are you ready to do this?" I ask.

She nods again, but she doesn't speak. She must be nervous.

I take her hand and she grips it much tighter than I expected. Does she want me to be there for her? Maybe she isn't as independent as she seems.

I head for the medical center entrance and I sense her falling behind my shoulder. I'm leading her and she lets me. That feeling eases some of my nerves. We're doing this together.

We go inside and I lead her up to the reception desk. Her voice shakes when she gives her name to the receptionist and then we both sit down in the waiting room.

She pulls out her phone and flips to a drawing app. She starts scribbling with her stylus and I look over her shoulder. "Are you working on the Hummingridge Mall project?"

She grins and blushes. "Drawing helps calm me down. Did you notice this spray of motion lines here?" She points to the trampoline sequence. "We should have those scatter and turn into birds."

"Good idea. We could have them scatter and turn into a bunch of different animals that go join different parts of the sequence."

I pull my smaller sketch notebook out of my jacket pocket. I wasn't sure if using it in the doctor's office would be inappropriate under the circumstances, but now that she's doing it, I can, too.

I take out a pencil and start sketching some cartoon animals that match the spray lines she mentioned. She laughs and points her stylus at a chubby elephant bouncing on the trampoline. "I love it!"

We go back to sketching and trading ideas. We both keep laughing so much that we get some dirty looks from a few old ladies who are waiting to be seen, but Juliet and I are having so much fun that we don't stop. We just make sure to keep our voices down.

We're working on some twisty transmutations for the jungle gym sequence when a young woman in scrubs comes into the waiting room. "Juliet?"

We both jump and scramble to put away our stuff. I take Juliet's hand and she practically crushes my fingers. She huddles much closer to me as we head into the back.

The doctor is a middle-aged woman with grey hair and plenty of wrinkles. There's only one chair by the doctor's desk. Juliet sits down while I stand next to her.

I see myself taking a defensive posture over her, but that seems right, too. I want to be that for her and the baby. I want to make sure everything's okay with her.

The doctor doesn't act like any of this is out of the ordinary. She smiles at me like I belong here as much as Juliet does.

The doctor starts bombarding Juliet with questions about her cycles and her symptoms and her daily habits. I listen extra close and take in every detail. I want to know everything there is to know about Juliet's daily life. I want to know if she's allergic to anything or if she has any problems with the pregnancy or if she needs help with anything.

The doctor finally waves to the exam table and tells Juliet to lie back and pull up her shirt. I ease over to her side while the doctor gets out the ultrasound machine.

I start watching the doctor when Juliet drops her hand to her side and seizes my hand in a death hold. She crushes it tight, and when I look at her, I find her staring up at me with huge eyes.

I react without thinking and stroke my other hand across her forehead to brush her hair back. I want to reassure her that I'm here. I won't let anything happen to her.

She doesn't seem to mind that or when I kiss the hand holding mine. This all seems normal somehow. I can hardly even remember that I'm not supposed to be doing any of these things. What else would I be doing with the woman who's having my baby?

My heart practically stops when the doctor squirts some gel on Juliet's stomach. I hold my breath as the doctor touches the wand to the gel and the machine comes on.

Juliet squeezes my hand so tight that I can't feel my fingers anymore, but I don't care. I want her to hang onto me. I want to feel that she's still here with me.

The doctor starts talking about what's on the screen, but I don't hear a word. I can barely think straight when she points to a round circle with a blob of some kind of gelatinous goo in the center. That's my baby. It's real. It's right there in front of me.

Juliet laughs and that sound snaps me out of my trance. I look down to find her beaming up at me and laughing. She looks so incredibly happy. Her other hand touches me and I realize that my free hand is gripping her shoulder too hard.

Maybe I'm not supposed to touch her like this, but she doesn't seem to care. She covers my hand and presses it deeper into her shoulder while she laughs at the image. Her eyes swivel up to mine and flood me with a tide of emotion. It hurts. I don't know if I can survive this feeling.

The doctor removes the wand from Juliet's stomach and the image cuts out. The doctor keeps talking about something or other, but I can't think. I hardly know where I am or what's happening while she hands Juliet a box of tissues to wipe the gel off her stomach.

Juliet pulls her hands away from me and I flounder in confusion trying to get my head back to reality. It's over. The ultrasound is normal. I don't have to worry about anything, but seeing that circle on the screen haunts my mind. I can't forget it. This is real. Juliet is pregnant and she's going to have my child. I'm going to be a father.

Juliet takes my hand and we walk outside together. I don't come back to Earth until we get back out onto the sidewalk outside. "Are you okay?" she asks me.

"Yeah. I'm fine." I can't look at her. I don't know if I'll ever be okay again—ever. Nothing will ever be the same after today.

"You're worrying me," she tells me. "You were fine before the ultrasound. What happened?"

I shake myself out of my fog and force myself to look at her, but I can't hold her gaze. "I'm okay. It's just.....so real."

She surprises me by putting her arms around me and hugging me. "It's wonderful. I am so grateful to you for this. I don't know how to thank you."

I don't know what to say so I just hug her back. Gratitude doesn't seem to cover how I feel about this. I don't know how I feel about this except that I feel.....changed. This changed me. I don't know who I am or what I am anymore. I don't know anything.

"Are we still going out on Saturday?" she asks.

I snap around fast and frown at her. "Of course we are! What made you think we weren't?"

"I don't know....just the way you're acting. You're a million miles away."

I force myself to cup her cheeks and kiss her. "I'm okay. I'm just...
..in shock, I guess. I wasn't expecting it to hit me like this."

Her face bursts with light and she opens her mouth, but she stops
herself from saying it and a shadow crosses her features. She glances
down at my mouth again and I have to kiss her.

She's right. I feel unimaginably grateful to her for giving me this. I
would never be able to repay her for this even as it hurts to feel that my
life will never be the same again.

Chapter 15: Juliet

Sophie sticks her head into my office breathing fast and talking a mile a minute. "Come out here quick, Juliet! Seriously! Come quick!"

"What's wrong?" I ask.

"Just come on!" she practically shrieks and darts away.

I get to my feet and stop dead in my tracks when I see Damian and the rest of his corporate board milling around the entrance to Animatrix's office. Some of them look lost, but Damian smiles at the animators who cower behind their monitors and try to pretend that he isn't there.

I pull myself together and walk over to them. "This is a surprise. What can I do for you all?"

"We'd like to talk to you, Juliet," Damian tells me. "In private."

"Uh...okay. Come on in." I usher them into the meeting room. Every animator on the floor gapes at me like I'm deliberately walking into the Maw of Death.

I shut the door and stand across the table from the board. "Have a seat. What can I do for you?"

Damian sits down first followed by his board members. I'm not sure I want to stand up, but I can't stay standing while they're all sitting.

"We would like to offer Animatrix a partnership deal with Masters Marketing," Damian begins. "Not a hostile takeover and not an acquisition. You and your current shareholders would all remain in place and your corporate structure and your staffing profile would all remain the same. You would continue to be independent and operate out of these premises....unless you decide that you want to change that."

I narrow my eyes at him. "What exactly are you suggesting?"

"A business partnership between Animatrix and Masters Marketing. Both of our corporations would continue to operate separately with no overlap, but Masters Marketing would have priority in your schedule for any projects we wanted you to undertake and we would ask a certain percentage discount on your rate as part of this partnership agreement."

"The work you did on the Hummingridge Mall campaign was spectacular," the vice-president tells me. "Truly impressive. We want that kind of talent in our organization, and if we can't acquire you, this partnership is the next best thing."

"And what would be the advantage for us?" I ask. "What could tempt us to give up whatever independence we already have to work for Masters Marketing?"

"The advantage to you would be a reliable stream of work," Damian replies. "You wouldn't have to go hunting for clients all the time, but you would be free to take whatever outside jobs come your way. You could work on all the same projects you're currently working on and even solicit new clients whenever you want, but you would always have a steady supply of work from Masters Marketing."

"Don't you already have your own animators?" I ask. "You already have teams of graphic designers working for you. Why do you need us?"

"None of our animators are as good as you," Damian replies. "We'll still keep our own design teams going to handle still copy, photography, sign design—that kind of thing. Everything moving and animated we'd like to outsource to you."

"So....." I choose my next words with care. "How much of a discount are you asking for?"

"Five percent," Damian replies, "and we would also offer you promotion space in all your returned product. At the moment, you're currently adding your logo to the lower lefthand corner of your final frames. We're offering a full-screen display of your logo animation and these extra few seconds will be billed to our clients under our contract budget. You would get the extra promotion of your service without any extra cost to you....except for the discount, of course."

I stare at him and the rest of the board vanishes out of my awareness. I can't believe I'm hearing this. The terms of this partnership agreement are beyond favorable. They're unheard of.

He must have done this. He came up with these terms....why? He isn't throwing me a bone and he isn't trying to trick me.

Is it possible that he really thinks Animatrix is good enough to be an equal partner in his company? All the rest of the board members smile back at me waiting to hear my answer. This is insane. They're seriously offering me this package.

I would never have to worry about finding clients again. I would never have to go hat-in-hand searching for investors. The extra work from Masters Marketing would put us so far into the green that I would never have to worry about money ever again.

Damian slides a folder across the table toward me. "All our terms are in here. You probably want to take a look at it and consult with your shareholders."

I glance toward the door. Most of the shareholders in this company are my employees. What will they say when they hear this?

"Ms. Holloway?" the vice-president asks. "Are you okay?"

"Yes!" I shake myself out of my trance. I have to struggle not to keep staring at Damian. He did this. He came up with this....for me. "Thank you very much for stopping by. I will call a shareholder meeting and we'll discuss your proposal in depth. Please let me know if there's anything I can do for you or if you need any more information on the company."

Damian breaks into a huge grin. "I think we have enough of that."

He stands up and the rest of his board does the same. I try to beat them to the door, but they're already filing out. Damian waits until last. His eyes shine with so much meaning and understanding. God, I want to kiss him for this!

I'll just have to wait until Saturday night. It seems like an eternity away.

I go back over to the table, sit down, bury my face in my hands, shut my eyes, and draw in a deep shuddering breath. What am I supposed to do about this?

There's only one thing to do and that's to take Masters Marketing's proposal to my shareholders.

That isn't the question on my mind, though. What am I supposed to do about Damian? I can already see him getting serious about this—about us. I'm getting serious about us, too. I just don't have the courage to show it the way he does.

I open the folder and flip through the pages. It doesn't say anything he and the board didn't already say. This is one hell of a proposal.

I sit there staring at the pages for so long that I lose track of time. All at once, the door pops open and Sophie sticks her head in. "Oh, my God! Are you okay, Juliet?"

"I'm fine, Sophie. I just needed to think."

She rushes over to me flapping her hands and whispering extra fast. "We wondered if you passed out in here or if the vampires drained your blood or something terrible like that."

I try to laugh, but it doesn't really come out. "They didn't."

I take the folder and leave the meeting room, but when I get out onto the office floor, I find every animator staring at me with the same stunned, petrified expression.

"What was that about, Juliet?" Ian asks in a shaky voice.

I wave the folder at nothing. "We need to call a shareholder meeting."

"What about?" Frank asks. "Is Masters Marketing buying us out after all?"

"Yeah," someone else chimes in. "Don't leave us in the dark, Juliet. Give it to us straight."

I squirm a few more times and bite the bullet. What am I waiting for? The people in this room own more stock than all the rest of the shareholders combined. If we decide to accept this proposal, we won't need to consult the rest of the shareholders.

I could make that call myself. I'm the controlling stockholder, but I couldn't do that to my staff. I couldn't go ahead with this without at least asking for their opinion.

"Masters Marketing wants to make us a business partner. They want priority in our project schedule and they want a discount on our rate in exchange for extra promotion and a steady supply of work. It means we would never have to worry about having enough clients....
.or money. We might even be able to expand and hire more animators depending on how much work they give us. We would still be totally independent with creative decision-making power and we would keep our own premises. Everything would be separate, but it would vastly

boost Animatrix's profile and would probably bring in a lot more work."

"But that's.....great!" Sophie remarks. "What's wrong with that?"

"I don't see anything wrong with it. It's a dream come true," I reply.

"But what about.....?" Ian begins and frowns. "So.....Mister Frosty the Snowman won't be our new boss?"

I take a second to realize that he's talking about Damian and I burst out laughing. "No, he won't be. I'll still be your boss....as long as you want me to be."

Dozens of voices chime in from all over the office. "Of course we do, Juliet!"

"No one could ask for a better boss than you!"

"Juliet for president!"

I laugh again and excited talk breaks out all over floor. Frank finally cups his hands to his mouth and bellows across the room. "Quiet!!" Everyone falls silent except for isolated giggling.

Frank turns to me. "You've been taking it on the chin for us for years, Juliet. Having a steady stream of work would be great for us, but it would be even better for you. If you say we should take this deal, then we should do it."

I can't help but beam at him. I love all my animators and the fact that they care about me enough to do this means so much more.

I look around the room. "So do we all agree? Does anyone object to this deal?"

Everyone looks around at everyone else. No one says anything.

"All right," I finally say. "It looks like we're doing this."

The room erupts in talk, jokes, and wild speculations about the future. I stand back and watch these people feeling an overwhelming rush of love for them all. I love Animatrix and I would do anything for them all. Is it possible that Damian feels the same way? Is that why he did this?

Chapter 16: Damian

I step up to the address that Juliet gave me, I ring the doorbell, and move back while I wait and survey the old house in a residential neighborhood. The house looks neglected and the paint is peeling from the old wooden siding.

Part of the gutter hangs down and weeds choke the flowerbed. The lawn has been moved but not edged. Is it possible that Juliet lives here of all places? Why would she live here when she can afford something so much nicer?

She comes to the door and I step back in to meet her. She comes out glowing. She's doing a lot of that lately. I'd like to delude myself a little longer that she's glowing because I'm here and not because she's pregnant.

She looks astounding in a sleek black dress that comes down to her knees. It has long sleeves and covers her skin and body. She doesn't have to show off because she's so damn hot that covering up makes her look even hotter.

The dress shows me all I need to see of her body, her curves, and her stomach. It's still flat, but it won't stay that way for long.

She blushes when she sees me. "Hi."

"Hi," I reply. "Are you ready to go?"

"Yeah." She steps out onto the porch, pulls the door shut, and locks it behind her. I wait until she finishes and take her hand before I lead her to my car.

Now I can take all the time I want to open her door for her and make sure she's sitting comfortably before I close it. I get behind the wheel and smile at her before I pull away from the curb.

"Are we going back to the Oak Street Kitchen?" she asks.

"I don't think that's a good idea after last time. I think we might get thrown out if you order the pickled pigs feet and I order the roasted perch with the head still on it."

She laughs, but it isn't her usually hearty guffaw. She giggles in a higher, girlish, I'm-going-on-a-date-with-this-guy way. "You're right. So where are we going?"

"Somewhere that they serve really boring food with no imagination." I glance over at her and take the plunge. "What's the story with that house of yours? It looks like it's haunted or something."

She laughs again. "It isn't haunted. It's just older than the dinosaurs—not really. I started renting it when I first moved to this city. I was just trying to make a living as animator and I couldn't afford anything else....and I guess I've just kept living there. I like it there and I never really wanted to spend more money to live somewhere less comfortable."

"So did you buy it? You could have fixed it up."

"I don't own it. I still rent it."

I stare at her and almost drive off the road. "You....what?"

She laughs at my reaction. "I know what you're thinking. I could have bought something nicer or fixed that up, but I kind of like it the way it is. It's got....character."

"It has more than that. It has a terminal illness."

She laughs again. "You wouldn't understand."

"Explain it to me." I take my hand off the wheel and move it over to hers to hold her hand while I drive. "I want to understand."

She blushes and looks away. She looks hypnotic when the street-lights flicker across her face and hair. "I like the house. I've been living there for so long that I'm comfortable there. It might not look like much from the outside, but the inside is homey. I feel relaxed and content there. I don't want to give that up. When Animatrix first started doing well and I started making more money, I told myself, 'Just stay where you are in case it doesn't work out'. I didn't want to move up in the world in case I just had to move back down again...so I stayed. After a while, when I realized that my circumstances would never go back down, I just kept staying. I feel at home there. I don't really want anything else, and if I did move, I would just be paying more for something that didn't make me feel at home."

I drive for a while thinking over everything she said. Nearly every conversation I have with her makes me think and reevaluate my life.

She brings me out of my thoughts by murmuring under her breath. "I knew you wouldn't understand."

"I do understand. That's why what you said is so powerful."

"How is it powerful? It's just the way it is."

"I guess I just never put into words how I feel....about everything."

"What do you mean?"

"You said my place was impressive. You said you couldn't imagine anyone living there and I said it was as good as anywhere else. I guess I never realized that the whole point of having something like that is to have a place you can call home. You said you couldn't imagine a child growing up somewhere like that and you're right. It's never been a home. I don't see how it ever could be a home. You can give the kid that, but I can't."

"Not necessarily," she replies. "You could make it a home. It's as much a home as you make it. My place wasn't a home when I moved in. It was a cold, hollow wreck with rotten carpet and moldy curtains. It only became a home after years of living in it."

"I've been living at my place for years and it's never been a home to me. It would never be a home for our child. I guess I should probably start looking for a place like that."

"Why should you? You could make it a home easily if you wanted to."

"How would I do that?"

"I don't know that because I don't know you well enough. Maybe it would become a home if you and the kid covered the walls in art."

I laugh and glance over at her. I don't want to look at the road. I want to keep looking into her eyes forever. I want to die in those eyes, but I have to keep driving.

"I'll tell you one thing," she goes on. "It will become a home when the kid leaves greasy fingerprints all over the walls and the fridge. It will become a home when the kid pukes on the carpet and wets the bed and smears mashed carrot all over your curtains."

I burst out laughing. I love that picture of my future. "Bring it on. I can't wait."

She laughs with me and squeezes my hand. We pull into the restaurant parking lot and I take her hand when I open the passenger door for her.

She walks close to my shoulder and her body brushes my side. She whispers in my ear, "We will definitely have to behave ourselves here. These people won't be nearly so forgiving of the Shrimpticles."

I snicker, but I don't laugh out loud. This is definitely not the Oak Street Kitchen. Nearly everyone wears fancy clothes and all the waiters wear tuxes and bowties. The tables are set with linen tablecloths, fine china, and crystal wine glasses.

"This must be where the Squares come to perform their mating rituals," I murmur back to her.

She giggles. "Is that what we are—Squares performing a mating ritual?"

I glance over at her and find her eyes glowing up at me. "I hate to tell you this, darling, but we already mated."

She laughs and her cheeks flush with rosy vitality. Holy fuck, I want to kiss her so bad!

Just then, the concierge takes the couple in front of us into the restaurant. It's our turn and he comes back for us. He leads us to our table in the back and Juliet blushes when I pull out her chair for her.

She leans her elbows on the table and tilts toward me. "Can I ask you something?"

"Sure. Ask me anything."

"My house....do you think it's good enough?"

"I don't know. I haven't seen the inside, but if you think it's good enough, then I'm sure it is. I trust your judgment on what's good enough for our child."

She colors again and dips her eyelashes. She smiles, but it isn't her usual impish grin. "I don't want you to think I would ever let our child live in a substandard house."

"Is it substandard?"

"I don't know. I've never had a kid before."

"Neither have I. I'm making this up as I go along." I hesitate and then blurt out, "Maybe you would consider my apartment a substandard living place for our child."

"Why would I think that? Your apartment is stunning. It's practically palatial."

I laugh, but this conversation is going in a direction I never expected. "Maybe you would think it was substandard because it's lifeless."

She opens her mouth and immediately looks away.

"It is, isn't it?" I go on. "It's lifeless. Say it."

"It's only lifeless because you don't make it a home. Maybe now that you have your drawings all over every flat surface, it's starting to become more of a home."

Now it's my turn to look away. I look down at the tabletop and see her hands lying there. I have to take them. I have to touch her. I can't stand being apart from her.

She looks down at my hands and murmurs under her breath. "I need to tell you something."

"Just don't tell me you want me to change the Shrimpticles' names. I spent five hours last weekend coming up with that name."

She doesn't laugh. She doesn't look up at me. "I.....want....."

I wait, but she doesn't go on.

"What's wrong, baby?" I breathe. "Tell me."

She looks up and her eyes latch onto me in an unbreakable grip. "This child.....needs....a home."

"I know that. That's why we're talking about my apartment being lifeless."

"I'm not talking about that." She took a deep breath. "I'm talking about.....a family. This child needs a family. This child needs a family that he or she can take the rainbow treasure chest home to after they find it on the Mountain of Mystery. Our child needs a home with two parents in it—a home where they're loved and cherished and supported and content."

I stare at her feeling the same overwhelming tide that nearly drowned me in the doctor's office.

"Say something," she murmurs. "You're scaring me."

I break her gaze with an almighty effort. "I know the child needs all that."

"Then you know that the child will be better off if we're a couple."

I nod. I can't speak. Is this really happening?

"I....want...." She chokes on the words. "I want us to be a couple .....not for the child....." She clamps her eyes tight shut and blurts out the words in a rush. "....but for me."

My blood turns to ice water. How did she have the courage to say those words?

Her voice strains to the breaking point. She sounds like she's crying, but she's just so pent up and tense that she can barely squeak out the words. "I need you....I need you to be there....for everything.....I need you to be......like that with me......I don't want to do this without you.....I want all the moments of this child's life.....to be just between us.....like the film.....I don't want to share that with anyone else.....I want to know that those moments......are like secrets between us......I want.....us to be that family.....you and me....."

She trails off breathing hard. Every word slaps me in the face. How have I been putting this off for so long? I should have been the one to say those words. I should have been the one to tell her how much I need her.

I can't look at her. I look down at her fingers laced in mine. I can only pray to God that she's looking at our hands, too, so she won't think I'm being disrespectful to her. "I need you, too. I need you to be that to me. I need you to show me how to make a house a home....and I need you to show me how to be the father this child needs. I need us to be a family....not for the child, but for me."

There. I said it. Now I can die feeling this everlasting need for her. I don't know what will happen to me if she turns me down. I'll probably fall apart. I feel like I'm falling apart right now.

She compresses my hand, and at that moment, the waiter comes over to us. "Good evening, folks," he says. "What can I get you to drink tonight?"

Juliet and I both look up at him and then at each other. The spell shatters and we're both back to normal except that we're both still holding hands.

I finally get my voice working. "We'll take a bottle of chardonnay and I'll have a gin and tonic."

"No problem." He lays the menus on the table and leaves.

I look over at Juliet to find her smiling at me. Those words hang in the air between us, but they don't crush me with their oppressive power anymore. They're out there in the world and no one can call them back, but it doesn't matter. She feels the same way I do. We both want the same thing.

She breaks into a full, conspiratorial grin as soon as the waiter leaves and she picks up the menu. "Let's see what they have here that we can turn into cartoon characters."

"See if they have any fried tarantulas and Laotian ant-egg soup."

She scans down the menu. "I think I'll play it safe and stick with good old-fashioned spaghetti and meatballs."

"Just don't start catapulting your meatballs across the restaurant and slurping your noodles to get the sauce all over your face."

She laughs and her eyes sparkle up at me. "Your apartment is definitely going to be the home that any child would love to grow up in."

I turn bright red and then get serious. "Okay. You just threw down a challenge. If we're doing this, if we're going to be a couple and make a house a home that this child is going to grow up in, shouldn't we be talking about living in the same place?"

She dips her eyelashes and then her eyes devour me with the same unstoppable power. "Okay. Let's talk about that."

"Which one of our places should we colonize—or should we get a completely new one?"

"I think I would feel self-conscious if you moved into my house," she replies. "I would feel like it wasn't good enough."

"If you don't want me moving into your house, the only question is how comfortable would you be moving into my apartment. I wouldn't want you to move into something that didn't feel like home to you."

"It would feel like home because you would be there......" She turns bright red. "And the child."

Those words make my heart soar. I'm a home to her. It would feel like home because I would be there.

"I want to give you that," I murmur. "I want to be home to you."

She gulps and her eyes moisten. God damn, she is so beautiful that I can't stand it.

I lean across the table and she leans in to kiss me. Our lips meet, and at that moment, the waiter comes back.

He sets down our drinks, picks up the menus, and takes out his notepad. "What can I get for you folks tonight?"

"I'm going to have the lamb chops and she's going to have the spaghetti with meatballs," I tell him.

Juliet explodes in a huge grin, but she doesn't make a sound until the waiter safely leaves. We never let go of each other's hands through the whole ordering process and we keep holding onto each other while we sip our drinks.

I keep gazing across the table at her. Home. She's going to be home to me and I'm going to be home to her. I love that. I love her. I don't have to hide it anymore.

"I have an idea," I murmur under my breath.

"Is it a cartoon character of a giant meatball with spaghetti for hair?"

I pretend not to hear. "After dinner, you come back to my apartment and see if we can turn it into a home."

She beams at me and compresses my hand. "I'm certain that we can."

Chapter 17: Juliet

Damian parks his car in the underground parking garage under his apartment building and I stop breathing when he turns to me. His eyes gleam with hidden fire. We're going upstairs to his apartment, not to have wild sex, but to make his apartment the home that our future family is going to live in.

My heart won't stop racing thinking about that. I told him everything—how I feel—how I need him.....God, I can't stop the adrenaline burning my insides when I remember those words. I need him. I need so, so much of him.

He slips his hand into mine and the world tilts on its axis when he leans in to kiss me. His kiss electrifies me with so much passion, but it's a different kind of passion. It's a passion for the future we're going to share.

He pulls back and gets out of the car without a word. He comes over to my door, opens it, and takes my hand to help me out of the car. Every move he makes sends a powerful message that he's doing it. He's becoming the man I need him to be. He's taking command of this whole situation exactly the way I need him to.

He shuts my door and leads me over to the elevator. He pushes the button and then tugs my arm to draw me over to him. He doesn't kiss me. He just looks down into my eyes....and knows.

He sees so much in me, so much I shudder to think about. He sees me in ways I've never even seen myself. He sees all my needs and wants and dreams and desires. He sees my hopes and prayers and fears and insecurities.

I swim in the vast depths of his eyes. Can I really handle the places he's taking me? Can I handle being the woman that needs him and leans on him and calls on him for help?

I want that more than anything. I see it all in his eyes. I only doubt it when I look away.

I hang onto his hand for dear life. I never want to let go in case I get lost in this sea of emotion. I can't survive without him. How did this happen?

The elevator dings and we step into the car. As soon as the doors close, he swivels in front of me and goes back to looking into my eyes. He looks all the way down to the bottom of my soul. He only moves to raise his hand and run his fingers down my cheek and makes me gasp when he reaches my neck.

The elevator stops and he breaks eye contact to lead me to his apartment—our apartment. Am I really going to come live here? Am I really going to make this place my home?

I step inside and he lets go of my hand to go off to do something. I don't see what he's doing or where he goes. He leaves me to wander alone through the apartment.

He leaves the lights low so I can see the view spread out to the farthest horizon. I see the apartment with new eyes, now that I'm actually considering coming to live here.

He's right. It's lifeless. It isn't a home. It's hardly even an apartment. It reminds me of a museum or maybe a train station. It's a place people pass through on their way somewhere else. Damian sat down on the couch the last time I came here. That might be the only time anyone has ever sat down on that couch. I can't imagine anyone sitting anywhere in this place.

Then I get a flashback of the words I said to him at the restaurant. This apartment is going to look very, very different with a child living in it. The kid is going to puke on the carpet and wet the bed and get greasy fingerprints all over the walls and smear mashed carrot all over the curtains.

I smile to myself when I think that. That would definitely make this place a home.

I go into the dining room and freeze on the threshold. Damian has changed it around since I was in here last. He's pushed the giant dining room table against one wall and brought in a whole bunch of other trestle tables. They surround the room hugging every wall and every single one of them is covering with colored-pencil drawings.

He's created sequences of several drawings that make up parts of stories. Five or six pictures lie in a row showing different parts of the story that he hasn't completed yet.

He must have at least twenty different stories started here, but most are incomplete and have sections missing, either at the beginning, in the middle, or at the end.

His characters are becoming even more idiosyncratic and the storylines better developed. I spend way too long going over them all and snickering at some of the facial expressions that tell the story so perfectly.

I'm nowhere near finished when Damian appears in the doorway holding a tumbler of gin and tonic in one hand and a glass of white wine in the other. "There you are. I thought you might have gotten lost in this mortuary."

I laugh. "These are awesome. You are definitely making something here."

"I just wish I could figure out what it is."

"I'm sure it will make itself clear very soon. Are you turning this dining room into your art studio?"

"It certainly looks that way, doesn't it?" He takes my hand. "Come in here."

He leads me back to the living room. "What are we doing in here?" I ask.

"We're kicking back at home." He kicks off his shoes, pulls off his socks, flops on the couch, and puts both feet on the coffee table.

I laugh, but when I still don't sit down, he pulls me down by my arm. "Sit down. Take a load off."

I sit down. "Now what?"

He reclines on the cushions and rests his gin and tonic on the arm of the couch. "Tell me everything about you."

"Can you be a little more specific?"

"Do you have any dietary requirements?"

"Yeah. I'm allergic to Squares."

He gasps and clutches at his heart. "Aarrghh! I'm hit."

I burst out laughing. "I didn't mean you."

"So have I changed enough? Am I not a Square anymore?"

"Definitely not. I'm not sure you ever were one."

"I was one when you first met me."

"I'm not so sure," I reply. "Maybe you were just undercover."

He laughs and takes a drink out of his glass. "It's good to know I'm out of the closet now."

I lean back on the cushions and find myself relaxing much more than I thought possible. "We're talking about me, not you. What else do you want to know?"

"What do you like to do on your days off when you aren't at work?"

"I don't usually take days off. There's only work at the office and work at home. I got in the habit of working on my projects at home on the weekends and I've just kept doing it."

"That has to change."

"What about you?" I ask. "What do you do on your days off when you aren't at work?"

"You mean what did I do before I got bitten by the art bug? I worked, of course."

He glances over at me and his eyes spark. All of a sudden, he extends his arm to me. "Come here. You're too far away."

He pulls me into his side and hugs me against his shoulder. I stiffen...and then relax. We're home. What else would we do at home?

I scoot over to his side and put my arms around his ribs. He kisses me on the head and I rest my head on his chest. This feels....incredible.

He presses his mouth to my hair and mumbles into my hair. "Do you like this?"

I nod. "It feels....like home."

He sighs and slouches down lower on the cushions. "Yeah. It does."

I hold him feeling this magical bliss. My house never felt like this. I've never felt this comfortable or content or happy anywhere ever.

I can almost feel what it will be like when we have kids running around making noise and messing things up. These moments will mean even more then. They'll be precious and rare. They'll be what makes this apartment a home.

I send up a silent prayer of gratitude that I decided to go through with this. Our child will see me and Damian holding each other like this. That's the most I want for our child—to see us together like this and loving each other.

I shut my eyes against those words, and the next second, I murmur, "I love you," into his chest. I don't want to hold anything back from him. I don't want to be with him without that between us, too.

He nuzzles into my head and his other hand clasps my cheek to hug me tighter to him. "I love you!" he whispers. "I love you more than anything!"

This pang of emotion in my heart hurts beyond measure, but it feels right. I hurt with love for him and for knowing that he loves me. He's so solid and comfortable. He would make any place home because he would be in it.

He cups my chin and raises my face to kiss me. His eyes consume me and then he says, "I love you," looking straight into my eyes.

Those words make my eyes sting with tears and then that feeling switches to pure joy. I burst into a huge smile and almost laugh out loud when I say, "I love you."

Loving him means joy and laughter and silliness and relaxation and peace. It means I'm right where I need to be and everything is perfect.

He tightens his arm around me and sweeps me off the couch. He picks me up, but instead of getting me to straddle him, he rotates me backward to sit sideways on his lap.

He cradles me in his arms. He's so big and protective and caring and strong. He rocks me on his lap and I feel how hard he is, but he doesn't explode in hot-blooded fury. His big, strong hands migrate over my body, but even the excitement of being with him feels easy and satisfying and peaceful.

He strokes my hair off my forehead, rubs the back of my neck, and then caresses down my arms before he starts fondling my breasts through my dress. Delicious pleasure floods me and carries me away to such a blissful place that I just relax and let it happen.

I hang onto his neck kissing him as deeply as I want while he explores my body. Everything he does makes me feel good, even as I sense him building up to the inevitable.

He squeezes and pinches my breasts through my dress until he makes me moan into his mouth. My body buzzes with desire and my tissues ache between my legs, but even that seems like part of all this.

He leaves my breasts and glides down to my hips. My body is his to explore. My pleasure is his and it excites him to know what I'm his to love, his to protect, his to delight.

He supports me with one arm while his hand slithers up my thighs under my dress. He finds my saturated panties and his fingers slide into me. I can't stop myself from dissolving in rapture on those fingers. Everything he does makes me surrender to his will. Being his is so deliriously, lusciously wonderful.

He tips my upper body back to give himself space to finger me as much as he wants. He never stops kissing me and he drinks the screams from my lips when he propels me to the highest heights. I don't fight him. I want him to carry me there on this cloud of ecstasy.

His hardness digs into me from below until I feel him throbbing. He wants it, but he never even takes his clothes off. He does everything for me and holds me suspended in this deep, satisfying place of offering everything to him.

I told him that I needed him and now he's delivering. He gives me the home I need and he becomes the man I need him to be. Whatever we might have done or been before no longer matters.

I open my eyes to find him gazing at me. His bottomless green eyes explore the inner recesses of my soul. Does he know what he's doing to me? Does he have a clue how much I need him?

He sweeps me off his lap, lays me down on the couch, and crawls up to my mouth to devour me in magical kisses. I wrap my arms and legs around him trying to pull him down on top of me. I want him to claim me and tell me that this baby is his. I want him to say that I'm his, too.

He kisses me, but he keeps his muscular frame above mine. He breaks off my mouth and crawls down my body biting and kissing me through my clothes. He dallies around my breasts for a while, but he doesn't try to get through my dress.

I sigh and moan when he teases me. Then, inevitably, he makes it all the way down to my legs and starts sliding my dress up as he kisses up my thighs. I quiver and spasm as he gets nearer to my saturated slit. I can't contain all the excitement and delirious sensation rushing through me.

He pushes my dress over to my hips and nuzzles into my panties. He hooks his powerful fingers around them, glides them down, and his torturous mouth devours me in such hot, succulent bites that I lose all control again.

I writhe on the couch trying to touch him while he consumes me to raving madness. I spasm and explode in his mouth as his tongue and fingers electrify me out of my mind.

He pulls my panties the rest of the way off and pushes my dress up while he mauls me to the ends of the earth. I pull my dress off over my head and unclip my bra, but he's too embedded between my legs to stop.

I collapse whimpering and shrieking on the couch while he rockets me to the stars. No amount of bucking and convulsing can stop the wave of pleasure and lustful desire taking me over. I want him so fucking bad. I want everything about him. I want him to demolish all my defenses and make me the woman who can share his life. My heart aches I want that so bad.

He crushes my thighs and ass in between fingering me to High Heaven. He reduces me to a quivering mass of nerves lying naked on his couch.

Just when I think he'll stay down there forever, he lifts off, gives me a few more masterful kisses right on my twitching mound, and pivots onto his hands and knees. He crawls up to my mouth, but he doesn't sink on top of me.

"Come upstairs with me," he growls. "I want you in my bed."

I hold onto him tight to steady myself from the power of those words. He wants me in his bed. He wants us to be a couple together in his bed—in our bed—in our family bed.

That's the place where our children will be conceived, the place where we'll cuddle and sleep in on Saturday mornings, the place where we'll both collapse after we come home from work. It's the place where we'll reconnect with each other after going out into the world.

He sits back and picks up my clothes for me. He does everything so casually even though he's as hard as a rock. He acts like we're already home—like I already live here. We're going upstairs to go to bed together. What could be more normal than that?

He stands up, takes my hand, and kisses me for ages. I'm naked in our living room and my body pulsates with all the sexual energy he excited in me, but that's okay. I'm with him. I'm his and we're going to bed together.

I never have to worry about him using me or taking advantage of the situation. Me being naked in his apartment can only mean one thing. I'm home and everything I do must be right. Nothing can ever be wrong here.

Chapter 18: Damian

I switch on the light in my bedroom and lead Juliet inside. She's magnificently naked and pliant after the pleasure I gave her on the couch. She follows all my movements exactly.

My God, she looks so immaculate like this! I want her more than ever, but I want her to be here more than anything. This gentle, effortless journey to my bedroom feels so destined and right. It makes me feel even better than sex even as I know that we're going to have the greatest sex of our lives as soon as we get into bed.

She sits down on the edge of the bed to wait for me while I lay her clothes on the chair. She watches me take off my jacket and put my shoes in the closet. Every passing second seems like it was chiseled out of time. How did I think I was ever going to avoid this?

This was always going to happen. It was written in the stars that first time I met her at the bar on the *Dream Dimension*. We were always going to wind up together. I just never imagined it would come to this—this blissful descent into inescapable gravity.

I go over to her and she puts her arms around my back when I cradle her cheeks. I kiss her, but the happiness of just looking down into her soft, loving eyes drowns out everything else. It even drowns out the desire to take her body.

She gazes back up at me with so much emotion and vulnerable need in her eyes. I want to show her through my gaze that I'm going to be the man she needs me to be. I don't want to hide from that responsibility anymore. I want those eyes to transform me into the man I could be.

I rake my fingers through her hair and then break away. I want to take my clothes off so we can get in bed. I won't be complete until I do that.

I turn away heading for the bathroom. She stands up and goes toward the head of the bed. She bends down to pull back the covers when, without warning, she slams down on her knees on the floor, hugs her arms across her stomach, and shrieks in pain.

I rush over to her as another shriek shatters my mind. "Baby!" I yell. "What's wrong?"

Screams answer me. She crunches over gripping both arms close to her abdomen. No. Please no. Don't let anything be wrong with the baby. I couldn't live with that.

I yell louder in her ear. "Juliet! Talk to me! What's happening?"

She's screaming too loudly to answer me, and when I look wildly around the room for any way to help her, she topples. She almost falls flat on her face on the floor, but I catch her just in time.

She lets out one broken scream after another and breaks down sobbing in between. She lies limp and helpless in my arms, but that's nothing compared to how helpless I feel.

I have to do something. I have to stop this from happening. I have to wind back the clock and turn our lives into the blissful, peaceful dream of just a few seconds ago.

I can't do that holding her like this. Her screams won't let me think. I slowly lower her to the floor babbling all about taking her to the hospital, but she doesn't hear me. She's crying too hard in between screaming in pain.

I stand up searching everywhere for my phone only to remember that I left it downstairs. I don't have time for that.

I jump over to the bed, yank the bedspread off, and wrap it around her. "Okay, baby," I gasp. "I'm taking you to the hospital. Everything's going to be okay. I got you."

Everything will not be okay, but I have to say something. I have to do something. I wrap the blanket around her and she bursts into sobs when I pick her up. She buries her face in my neck and bawls her eyes out while I take her downstairs.

"Don't....let anything...happen to the.....baby, Damian," she whimpers. "Please.....don't let anything......happen to the baby."

"Okay, baby." I kiss her on the forehead fighting down panic and despair. Her voice destroys my last nerve.

Nothing better happen to this baby. It can't. The baby has to be all right. It has to. I can't survive if anything happens to it.

She wakes me up fast with another scream and then dissolves in tears when I step into the elevator. Everything is taking way too long. I need to get her help right now.

I put her in my car and grit my teeth for the longest drive of my life. She keeps shrieking in the passenger seat and then exploding in loud wailing sobs. Those noises threaten to shatter me out of my mind. What if I lose her and the baby? I would be finished if that happened.

I screech into the hospital parking lot, pick her up, and carry her inside. Nurses surround me and take Juliet away from me. They put her on a stretcher and turn away to start wheeling her into the back when she lunges off the bed, shoots out a hand, and grabs me.

"Don't leave me, Damian!"

She hangs onto me and tows me with her while the medical people take her away. They're all talking fast and giving orders in all directions. A few people ask me questions, but I'm too stunned and devastated to answer very well. I don't even know if she's allergic to anything.

I can't lose her or the baby, not now, not after we just made the decision to go forward as a couple.

They finally park Juliet in a cubicle, hook her up to a million wires, and most of the medical people go off somewhere else.

Juliet turns her tear-streaked face up to me. "Don't let anything happen to the baby, Damian!" she wails. "Please.....don't let anything happen to it!"

I swivel over to her side and take her in my arms, but I want to cry right now. This can't be happening. "I love you, baby. I love you so much."

I don't know what else to say. I don't want to let anything happen to the baby, but there isn't a lot I can do. In fact, there's nothing I can do. I'm totally helpless to stop this disaster from wiping out my life and hers.

I hug her tight and she sobs on my shoulder crushing me in her arms. How did tonight turn from such a dream come true into this nightmare?

A young male doctor comes over to Juliet's bed wheeling an ultra-sound machine. "Let's just get that blanket off you and we'll see how everything's going with your baby."

He sounds way too nonchalant about this. He doesn't seem to realize that the world is ending.

I don't want to let go of Juliet. I want to keep holding her in my arms forever—as if that could somehow save us from what's about to happen.

I don't want to hear what the doctor finds out about what's happening with our baby. I don't want to hear that it's all over.

The doctor starts to unwind the blanket from around Juliet's naked body. She looks so small and frail and helpless buried in her nest of blanket.

I get pushed to the side, but I don't want to stand off in the cold while she goes through this alone.

I sit down on the edge of the bed and put my arms around her as the doctor squirts gel on her stomach. Juliet turns to me and cowers against my shoulder while we both wait for the verdict.

I'm supposed to be the bigger, stronger one. I'm supposed to be the one protecting her from all harm, but I can't protect her from this. I can't even protect myself from the impending catastrophe that will wipe out everything that I am.

I kiss the top of her head. How pathetic and useless all those tokens of affection are compared to this.

The doctor touches the wand to her stomach and the same grainy image appears on the screen. He locates the ball of goo and murmurs under his breath. "Hmm. Yes. The placenta appears to be partially separating from the uterine wall which explains the pain you're experiencing. The rest of the attachment appears to be solid and holding."

I gulp down the urge to get hysterical. "What does that mean? Is she going to lose the baby?"

Juliet breaks down crying into my shirt and I hug her tighter. Someone has to hold it together just long enough to find out our fate.

"The separation is only partial at this point. We'll keep it under observation and we can give her some medication to slow and hopefully arrest the rate of separation, but right now, we just have to wait and see."

He leaves taking his machines with him and Juliet crumples in my arms. I wrap the blanket back around her, but that isn't enough. I climb onto the bed and fold her in my arms as we both lie back on the pillows.

She keeps sobbing while I trail my fingers through her hair and kiss her on the forehead, but I can't think of anything to say. Nothing comes close to describing how devastated I feel.

I can't lose this baby. I can't lose all the happiness and possibility this baby brought to my life. This baby changed everything about me and woke me up from a deep sleep. I can't lose that. I can't go back to being lifeless and bloodless and heartless the way I was before. I'd rather die.

All at once, Juliet raises her head and looks at me through her eyes brimming with tears. Her blotchy face expresses all the anguish and heartbreak that I can't let myself feel right now.

"What's going to happen, Damian?" She chokes and then breaks down in wretched sobs. "What's happening to me?"

"I'm here, baby." I fight down despair and pet the tears off her cheeks. I need to take care of her. That's the only way I can get through this. "I'm with you. We're in this together. Whatever happens to you will happen to me, too."

She forces herself to look up at me and tears pour down her cheeks. "If we lose this baby.....Does that mean.....we lose us, too?" She bursts into loud sobs. "Do we lose the home and the family, too? Is it all over and gone?"

"Nothing's gone, baby." I fight down tears, but they come anyway. They sting my eyes and I can't hold them back anymore. "We'll always have the home and the family. We'll always have the rainbow treasure chest, and if we lose this baby, we can always try again. We'll just keep trying until we build the home we want."

Her mouth twists in all the wrong directions and her face keeps screwing up with anguish. "You promise?"

"I promise." I fold her in my arms and kiss the side of her head. I need that promise as much as she does.

I need to know we'll still be able to go home when this is all over. I need to know that she'll still be my family. I won't go home to an empty apartment and a blank future with me just stumbling around in the wasteland of my own pathetic existence.

We both lie back on the bed and I try to force myself to relax. This is not what I had in mind for ending our evening curled up in bed together, but I'll take it. She's here with me. We're together, and whatever this night holds for us, it will end with us being a family. I can live with that.

Chapter 19: Juliet

I wake up in Damian's arms, but this raw, battered feeling tells me we didn't just spend a night of bliss and connection in his apartment. I'm in the hospital and I might lose my baby.

He lies on the hospital bed next to me, sound asleep. He still wears the same clothes he had on during our date. He hasn't moved all night and he has his arms wrapped around the bedspread from his apartment.

I try to relax, but this endless waiting wracks my nerves to the breaking point. I need to know if my baby will be all right, but in a way, it doesn't matter anymore.

He said we would be a family together no matter what happened with this baby. He said we would try again if we lost it.

I can survive this disaster knowing that he's here. Everything we built before last night is still there waiting for me when I get out of the hospital. I won't be facing an endless future alone and destroyed.

His embrace makes me feel small and protected and safe even in this nightmare. I thank God he's with me and that our relationship developed the way it did. I couldn't face this alone. I couldn't survive going home to an empty house after pinning all my hopes and dreams on this baby.

I'm not sure I would ever be able to animate anything again, either. I would constantly be thinking about the film I made for this baby and I would always ache for the child that would never see it.

I don't feel that way with Damian here. He shares my agony over the possibility of losing this baby. This is just one more moment, one more secret memory that only he and I will share. No one ever has to know we went through this, but we'll know every time we look at each other.

He makes it all okay. We'll try again. We'll keep trying until we build that home the way he says. We'll have a child who can see that film and who will fill our lives with joy. It's only a matter of time.

Some child will see that film. It might not be this child, but someone will. Someone will paint their pictures on the apartment wall and decorate the apartment with stains, smudges, and fingerprints.

I shut my eyes and relax into his arms thinking about that. That beautiful vision will get me through this thanks to him. He gave me that. He's such a blessing on my life. I never imagined a man could do this for me, but he's right here. He's been with me all night and he'll never go away. He's my rock and I love him for that.

I thought I would be spending the night in his arms. I just thought I would be doing it in his apartment, not in the hospital. This horrific ordeal almost makes it worth it to get him. I never would have had him like this if we didn't go through this together.

I wish I could sit up and look at his face right now. I wish I could watch him sleep and admire how talented and protective and considerate he is, but I can't do that without waking him up. I couldn't do that to him, not after he showed up for me like this.

I shut my eyes and try to relax when the curtain around my bed rips back. The same doctor from yesterday comes toward me checking his clipboard. "Well, Ms. Holloway, we've checked your ultrasound results and it looks like your placenta isn't separating any more than it was when you came in last night. We're going to prescribe you an oral form of the same medication we've been giving you since you came in and you can keep taking it at home."

I blink at him. "You mean...you're sending me home? My baby isn't in danger?"

"No, I'd say the placenta will reattach in time and you can...."

Damian raises his head, sniffs, and squints into the blinding fluorescent lights. "What's happening?"

"The doctor says the baby isn't in danger anymore. They're sending me home."

Damian blinks a few times, frowns, and then looks at me. Our eyes meet and he bursts out laughing. I can't help but join in when he throws his arms around me and collapses on my shoulder, laughing in relief.

The doctor scowls at our reaction, taps his pen on his clipboard, and clears his throat. "As I was saying, the placenta should reattach in a few weeks and we'll check the fetus's heartbeat and blood supply at your next ultrasound."

Damian explodes in laughter, hugs me, and kisses the side of my head. Tears spring to my eyes, I'm so relieved. I hug him back. Everything's okay! I'm going home.

The doctor writes me out a prescription for the drugs and leaves after telling us that the nurses with arrange my release paperwork.

As soon as the doctor leaves, I turn to Damian and we both start laughing. I throw my arms around him feeling such an unstoppable tide of love and relief that I can't let go of him.

He hugs me back, and when he laughs in my ear, it sounds like he's crying. I crush him against me. I never want anything to come between us again.

We're okay. We're going home. I'm still pregnant and we're still together. We're still a family. He straightens up and I look into his eyes brimming with tears, but he smiles so broadly and so happily. He looks excruciatingly beautiful like this.

He runs his wrist across his nose and sniffs. "Come on, baby. Let's get the hell out of here. We're going home."

I sit up, but it's a little tricky getting out of the hospital when I'm still stark naked. Damian asks one of the nurses who gives me a pair of white pajamas. That's good enough for me.

Damian takes my hand and we walk out to his car. We stop by the pharmacy on our way home and he goes inside and gets my prescription for me since I'm not dressed well enough to go out in public.

He comes back to the car and kisses me, puts the prescription in my hand, and fires up the car. I don't want to talk or even kiss until we get home.

He parks in the underground parking garage and we hold hands in the elevator on the way up to his apartment. He puts his keys on the table by the door and collapses on the couch. "Let's not do that ever again. I can't take it."

"It's a deal." I sit down next to him and lean against him. "Where were we when we were so rudely interrupted?"

He puts his arm around my shoulder and pulls me in. "Right about here." He kisses me on the forehead and eases me down on his chest.

He gives a long, shaky sigh when I lay my head on his chest and wrap my arms around him. "I love you so much."

He groans and breathes into my hair. "Baby! I was so worried about you. I couldn't survive if anything happened to you."

I don't have to doubt that anymore because I feel the same way about him. I can't live without him and I don't want to try.

He puts both arms around me and crushes me in an almighty hug. His big body protects me from my worst fears. I can get through anything as long as I'm with him.

He rotates to one side, stretches out on the couch, and pulls me in next to him. Now we can both relax and never move again, but at that moment, a phone trills in the background.

Damian raises his head and frowns across the apartment. "What the hell is that?"

"It's my phone. I left my handbag over there when we came home last night." I start to get up to go get it from the kitchen, but he gets up first.

He brings it back and hands it to me before he sits down in the same place. I pull out my phone and relax when I check it. "Who is it?" he asks.

"Frank has a question about his current project. I better call in sick."

"You aren't going to work this morning," Damian tells me. "Don't even think about it."

"I won't. I just need to tell everyone that I won't be coming into the office."

"Will they ask any awkward questions?"

"You mean about why I'm moving into a top-floor penthouse apartment across town and wearing clothes that are four sizes too big for me? They'll ask awkward questions sooner or later and then it will be confession time."

"What will you tell them?" he asks.

"The truth, of course."

"What will they say when they find out you're pregnant?"

"They'll be thrilled that I'm pregnant. They'll be horrified when I tell them that I'm becoming the pampered house pet to the Prince of Darkness."

He bursts out laughing. "I guess I made an impression on them when this all got started."

"You certainly did." I send Frank a return text explaining that I won't be coming into work today. I don't give the details. "You might have started to change that with your partnership offer."

"You said the employees were favorable. You said they agreed to it."

"They did, but they still didn't want Frosty the Snowman to be their boss."

He laughs, gets to his feet, and takes my hand. "Come here, baby. We have somewhere we need to be."

He takes me back upstairs to his bedroom. It's still a mess after last night and the bed doesn't have a bedspread on it anymore.

He throws the one I wore to the hospital into the laundry basket and pulls a clean one out of the closet. He flips it over the bed and quickly makes the bed before he pulls down the covers.

He comes over to me and his eyes tell me exactly where it is that we need to be. He strokes my cheeks and feasts his eyes on my face. "I love you, baby," he croaks. "I never want you to be anywhere except right here."

I sink into his kiss. I can't make a joke out of this. We'll have plenty of time for that before this is all over.

I sway in the gravity of his kiss and then he steps back. He holds me captive with his eyes while he lifts my pajama shirt over my head. He drops it next to the chair and then kneels down when he slides down my pants.

He leaves me naked the way I was last night and I tremble when I see him recreated every step we went through before I went to the hospital.

He gives me one kiss right between my legs before he gets to his feet, leads me to the head of the bed, and sits me down. He eases me back and tucks me under the covers before he brings the blankets and bedspread up to my chin.

He kisses me on the forehead, straightens up, and starts unbuttoning his shirt exactly the way he did last night, but it means something different this time. He doesn't wander around the room. He just stands there devouring me with his unbroken gaze.

He strips off his shirt and my stomach clenches when he starts taking off his pants. His chest and shoulders strain with muscle and I can't stop staring at him in mounting desire. I want him. I want everything that's going to happen between us when he gets into this bed with me.

He goes around to the other side of the bed, pushes off his pants as he sits down, and kicks off his shoes. I can't keep away from him when I see the muscles of his back rippling and flexing with every move.

I drag my fingers up and down his spine, and when he still doesn't turn around, I wrap my arms around his waist and kiss his back and sides. I want every part of him.

I want him in bed with me. I want to cuddle and fall asleep and wake up and do it some more before we both pass out in exhaustion. I want to fool around and crack jokes and trade ideas for our drawings and talk about business and everything else.

He has to break my grip when he finally turns around and crawls under the blankets with me. He positions himself on the pillows and we both sink into a bottomless cloud of relaxation when we finally lock our bodies together.

I hug his midsection and rest my head on his chest while he hugs me around the shoulders. We both keep sighing and groaning in so much blissful relief and relaxation that we're finally here. We're home and we're in our own bed. Nothing can ever be bad again.

I kiss his chest, and once I start, I don't want to stop. I sneak lower and kiss his stomach. I love his body and I want to spend an eternity kissing every inch of him.

I rotate on top of him and lie down between his legs. This is mine. This man is mine to love, mine to worship, mine to pleasure, mine to hold, mine to make happy. I don't have to rush. I can take all the time in the world to make him happy and make myself happy at the same time.

Epilogue: Juliet

I turn off the stove and move down the kitchen counter to check a notification that pops up on my tablet. It's from Phoebe Mc-Cleod, the design manager from Masters Marketing. She's sending through a bunch of new jobs for Animatrix and wants my feedback on the client's initial concept suggestions.

High-pitched laughter makes me look up. My toddler son Jake stands at the coffee table in the living room with a vast sheet of paper spread out on the tabletop in front of him. Crayons and colored pencils cover the paper along with scribbles, doodles, and plenty of colored and greasy fingerprints.

He points to the TV screen in front of him where Little Boy Jake dances and bee-bops across the landscape on his quest to reach the Mountain of Mystery. He's coming to the part where the Shrimpticles are swimming and undulating across his path and trying to convince him to join them on the Great Migration to their mating grounds.

"Funny!" My son points to the screen, laughs in a shrill squeak, and looks at me to make sure I get the joke. "Funny!"

"Yeah, it's funny, isn't it?"

Evidence of our shared existence covers every inch of this apartment—literally. One whole giant wall of the apartment displays

Damian's brightly covered cartoon characters, ridiculous landscapes, and zany storylines.

Framed modern art used to cover the adjacent wall when I first moved into this apartment. Now Damian has taken all of that down and rearranged the furniture so that wall is blank, too. It's blank except for the pencil sketches of pictures he plans to paint on that one, too.

We're back to having a real dining room again, now that he's moved his art studio into our spare bedroom. The dining room looks nothing like it used to, though, now that a toddler eats there every evening.

Jake laughs again and points at the screen. He jumps up and down when he sees one of his favorite parts of the film—a giant monster that threatens the Shrimpticles in their Great Migration.

The monster is really just a giant head sticking out of the ground. Its enormous mouth yawns open and several Shrimpticles have to swim madly to escape getting swallowed.

I laugh at the monster's facial expressions. Maybe when Jake gets older, he'll recognize how similar the monster looks to Damian...or maybe that little joke will remain a private secret between me and Damian.

I don't mind if it does. Jake loves that film even if he's too young to understand the message about taking the rainbow treasure chest home to his family.

Damian comes downstairs just then and goes over to the fridge. "Watch out for the Brundle Monster, son," he calls across the living room when he sees what Jake is looking at.

I laugh again and look back down at my tablet. I'm scrolling through Pheobe's email when I get a notification from....I freeze when I see that it's from Bart Everette at Paper Tiger Film Studios.

Jake yells, "Funny!" again, but I don't look up. My gaze rivets to the email and Damian comes up behind me.

He slips his arms around my waist and rakes his fingernails down my thighs when he pulls me backward against him. He burrows into my neck and nibbles up to my ear....and then he freezes, too, when he sees what I'm looking at.

Hi Juliet

We absolutely loved your storyboard concept and your original art. We would love to offer you a contract to continue making this new animated film with your mysterious collaborator. We're all in stitches to find out who it is, but I suppose you'll have to unmask the secret stranger when you come in to sign the contract. When can we make an appointment to discuss the terms? We'd love to offer you the same advance and residual split as your last film. Just between us, I think the studio would be very favorable to raising your rate if you really insisted on it, but we can discuss all that at our initial meeting. Contact my assistant to arrange a time that works for both you and your Man of Mystery.

Yours, Bart.

The attached storyboard drawings showing mine and Damian's concept art peek out from the bottom of the email. They show Damian's expert colored pencil shadings highlighted with a few CAD enhancements.

Damian presses his mouth to my ear. "I'm your Man of Mystery, baby. Would you like it if a secret stranger crawled into your bed tonight and explored your body until you scream with delight?"

I gasp in rising desire when he drags his fingertips down the front of my legs again and then shifts them to the back to scratch up the backs of my legs to my ass.

"Mommy—look!" Jake shrieks and bursts into more laughter as the film moves on to the Land of the Squares.

Damian kisses my cheek from behind and shoves me hard against the kitchen counter, but I can't show how much he turns me on. I have to behave myself when Jake is around.

I pick up my tablet, swipe to a different email, and hold it up where Damian can see it. I count down the seconds while he reads it.

It shows the results of my latest pregnancy test—the positive results.

Damian buries his face in my neck one more time and his hand glides down to my stomach. He grips my stomach so lovingly and I shut my eyes into his powerful embrace. Our family is about to get a little bigger, a little crazier, and a little more wonderful.

Damian and I will become more successful, more creative, and more deeply in love with every passing day. We might even need a bigger apartment to accommodate all the rainbow treasure that every member of our family will be bringing back here to celebrate with us.

<u>The End.</u>

If you enjoyed this book, please consider leaving a review. You can also support me on Patreon at <u>www.patreon.com/InvisiblePublishing</u>.

Sign Up Once--Get all A.E. Moran's free books including brand new releases

When Doctor Lily Rice moves into a small mountain town to live in isolation away from the world, she sets off a chain of events no one could predict. Her arrival throws town doctor Parker Davis into turmoil. Is Lily trying to steal his patients and drive him out of practice.....or is there something much more sinister at work here?

The two get thrown together by circumstance and fate, only for secrets from both their pasts to threaten everything they've worked to build. Can two broken strangers find happiness through devastation before disaster tears them apart?

Sign up at www.authoraemoran.com to read it for free.

About AE Moran

A.E Moran is the contemporary romance pen name for Theo Mann.

I write 70 books per year—and yes, before you ask, all these books are my original creative work. Nothing written under my name is AI-generated or ghostwritten because I write better than AI and any ghostwriter out there.

People don't read fiction for entertainment or to escape from reality. People read fiction to see their humanity reflected in another person's character and story.

This is my promise to you. When you read my books, you'll see your own humanity reflected in the characters and stories. I take this commitment to my readers very seriously. My books are an intimate form of communication between us. I would never disrespect my readers by turning that over to a machine or another writer. This is my bond between me and you as my reader.

I write 20,000 words per day as my daily work output. If anyone with a public platform would like to challenge me to prove this in a controlled environment, feel free to contact me on this website's contact page. How do I do write so much? Find out more on my blog, *Crimes Against Fiction* at www.theomann.com.

I worked as a professional ghostwriter for fifteen years. Now I'm going for the Guinness World Record by writing 700 books over the next ten years and 1400 books over the next twenty years, all originally written by me.

See my website for the full book list. I'm also the author of *Proof for the Existence of God* and the *Crimes Against Fiction* blog.

You can find out more at www.theomann.com or at www.author aemoran.com.

Also by AE Moran (so far)